DAWNLANDS

DAWNLANDS

DAWNLANDS

A Novel

PHILIPPA GREGORY

THORNDIKE PRESS
A part of Gale, a Cengage Company

Copyright © 2022 by Vivat Publishing Ltd.
The Fairmile Series #3.
Family tree designed by Jill Tytherleigh.
Thorndike Press, a part of Gale, a Cengage Company.

Thorndike Press® Large Print Basic.
The text of this Large Print edition is unabridged.
Other aspects of the book may vary from the original edition.
Set in 16 pt. Plantin.

LIBRARY OF CONGRESS CIP DATA ON FILE.
CATALOGUING IN PUBLICATION FOR THIS BOOK
IS AVAILABLE FROM THE LIBRARY OF CONGRESS.

ISBN-13: 979-8-8857-8319-4 (hardcover alk. paper)

Published in 2022 by arrangement with Atria Books, a Division of Simon & Schuster, Inc.

Printed in Mexico
Print Number : 1   Print Year : 2023

DAWNLANDS

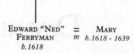

EDWARD "NED" = MARY
FERRYMAN m b.1618 - 1639
b.1618

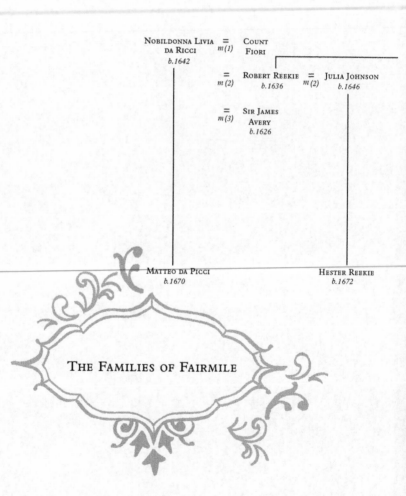

NOBILDONNA LIVIA = COUNT
DA RICCI m (1) FIORI
b.1642

= ROBERT REEKIE = JULIA JOHNSON
m (2) b.1636 m (2) b.1646

= SIR JAMES
m (3) AVERY
b.1626

MATTEO DA PICCI   HESTER REEKIE
b.1670   b.1672

THE FAMILIES OF FAIRMILE

THE FERRYMAN FAMILY

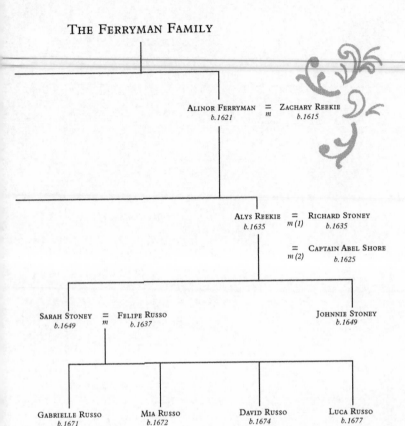

ALINOR FERRYMAN = ZACHARY REEKIE
b.1621 *m* *b.1615*

ALYS REEKIE = RICHARD STONEY
b.1635 *m (1)* *b.1635*

= CAPTAIN ABEL SHORE
m (2) *b.1625*

SARAH STONEY = FELIPE RUSSO
b.1649 *m* *b.1637*

JOHNNIE STONEY
b.1649

GABRIELLE RUSSO
b.1671

MIA RUSSO
b.1672

DAVID RUSSO
b.1674

LUCA RUSSO
b.1677

Northside Manor, Yorkshire,
Spring 1685
Livia Avery came down the grand staircase of Northside Manor in a tailored black velvet riding habit, her gloved hand lightly on the bannister, the heels of her riding boots clicking on the polished wood. Her husband, Sir James, crossing the stone-floored hall, looked up and noted the letter in her hand and the flush in her cheeks.

"So, you finally get your wish," he said levelly. "You've waited most patiently. It's been five years since you met the duchess, and now she is queen. I thought you had given up."

She took a little breath. "I never give up." She showed him the royal seal.

"Is it a royal summons?"

"We can't speak here!" she ruled and led the way into the library. Large logs smoldered in the hearth; she undid the mother-of-pearl buttons on her dark riding jacket and pulled at the cascade of fine lace at her throat. He observed her beauty with nothing but weariness. She was like the classical statues she had dotted around his house and gardens — lovely to look at, but meaningless to him.

She sat in the great chair before the fire, leaning slightly forward, her face glowing in the firelight as if posing for a portrait. Her hair was still glossy black, the creamy skin smooth on her cheeks, a few light lines around her dark-lashed eyes. She waited for him to take his seat opposite her before she would speak.

"I'm all ears," he said ironically.

"I am summoned to court," she breathed. "James, Duke of York, is to be crowned king, his wife is queen. There is no support for the late king's bastard. James the Second will inherit without challenge, and my dearest friend Mary of Modena will be queen." She was as exultant as if she had herself persuaded the people of England to crown the unpopular Roman Catholic brother to the king, instead of the adored Protestant bastard son. "She writes that she needs me, she is unwell. I will, of course, obey."

Still he said nothing.

"You could come with me? I am to be a lady-in-waiting, we could open Avery House? I could get a place at court for you. This could be a fresh start for us."

He cleared his throat. "I'm not sure that I

want a fresh start. I doubt that I'd want anything you can give me."

Her dark eyes flashed with irritation. "You cannot expect me to refuse a royal invitation; it's practically a command."

He turned his face from her show of temper. "Really? I imagine that you could very well refuse. But I am absolutely certain you have courted her — writing every week, sending little gifts, all your engaging tricks — I imagine you have begged her to invite you. And now: she does."

"You should be grateful to me . . ."

"You can go." He had no interest in what she might say. "I will send you in the carriage. I imagine you will live at St. James's Palace while they rebuild Whitehall. I assume you will return here when they go to Windsor in the summer?"

"You agree?" she demanded.

He shrugged. "You may do as you wish. As always. You are aware that the court is famously —" He broke off, searching for the right word. "Extravagant," he said. "Corrupt," he added. "Lascivious. But you will not mind that."

She raised her eyebrows as if in disdain; but her face was pale. "You can hardly think that I —"

"No, I believe that you are quite above weakness. I am quite sure you will lock your bedroom door in London as you do here.

11

Perhaps there, you will have reason."

"Of course, my reputation will be without stain."

"And you should be discreet in the practice of your faith."

She tossed her head. "Her Grace — I should say Her Majesty — and I are proud of our shared faith," she said. "She will open the royal chapel in St. James's Palace. She is appointing the Benedictine order —"

"London will not tolerate Roman Catholics practicing religion in public," he told her. "You may attend the queen's oratory inside the palace, but I advise you not to show off in chapels outside the palace walls. There's bound to be trouble, perhaps even worse than we've had already. Their Majesties should be as discreet, as the late King Charles."

"We're not all turncoats!" she flashed.

"I renounced my Roman Catholic faith to live my life as an English gentleman," he said steadily. "The Church of England is my faith; not a failing."

She thought his whole life was a failure: he had changed his faith; he had betrayed his first love; Livia herself had played him for a fool, and trapped him into marriage for his name and fortune.

"I am Roman Catholic," she told him proudly. "More so now than ever. All of England will return to the true faith, and it is you who will be in the wrong."

He smiled. "I do admire how your devotion increases with the fashion. But you had far better be discreet."

She looked at the fire, the heavy wooden carving of his coat of arms on the mantelpiece, and then to him, her dark eyes melting, a little smile on her lips. "James, I want to talk to you about my son."

He settled himself a little deeper into his chair, as if he would dig his heels into the Turkey rug.

"Once again, I ask you to adopt him and make him your heir."

"And once again, I tell you I will not."

"Now that I am bidden to court —" she began.

"He is no more my son than he was before. And I doubt you were bidden."

"He has been educated at the best schools in London, he will eat his dinners at the Inns of Court, he is being raised as an English gentleman by the family that you chose for him. You can have nothing against him."

"I have nothing against him," he agreed. "I am sure he is being raised well. You left him with a family of high morals and open hearts. He can visit you in London if you wish — but you may not go to the warehouse and see them, his foster family. You may not disturb them or distress them. That was agreed."

She folded her lips on an angry retort. "I've no wish to see them. Why would I go down-

13

river to a dirty wharf? I don't wish to speak about them, I never even think about them! It is Matteo! We are talking about my son, Matteo . . ." She put her hand to her heart.

Unmoved, he watched her dark eyes glisten with tears.

"I have sworn that unless you make him your adopted son and heir, I will conceive no other," she reminded him. "My door will stay locked as we grow old, childless. I will never disinherit my boy. You will never have a legitimate son if you do not first give my son your name. You will die without a legitimate son and heir!"

He barely stirred in his chair, though she had raised her voice to him. "You do know that I have rights to your body by law?" he confirmed. "But — as it happens — I do not assert my rights. There was never any need for you to lock your bedroom door. I don't want to come in."

"If you want to live like a priest!" she flamed out at him.

"Rather a priest than a fool," he replied calmly.

She put her hand to the back of her neck, pinning back one of the dark ringlets that fell over her collar. She made her voice warm and silky. "Some would say you are a fool not to desire me . . ."

He looked at the flames of the fire, blind to the seductive gesture. "I was led down that

14

road once," he said gently. "Not again. And you're what? Forty-five? I doubt you could give me a son."

"I'm forty-two," she snapped. "I could still have a child!"

He shrugged. "If I die without an heir, then so be it. I will not give my honorable name to another man's son. An unknown man at that."

She gritted her teeth, and he watched her fight her temper. She managed to smile. "Whatever you wish, husband. But Matteo has to have a place of his own. If he cannot be an Avery of Northside Manor, then he has to be da Picci of Somewhere."

"He can be da Picci of Anywhere; but not here. I have nothing against the boy, and nothing against you, Livia. I acknowledge you as my wife and him as your son. You won my good name when you deceived and married me, but that was my own folly and I have paid for it. Your son will not enter into my estate, but he is free to make his own fortune if he can, or batten off you if he cannot."

"If you're still thinking of her and her child . . ."

His face showed no emotion. "I have asked you not to speak of her."

"But you think of her! Your great love!"

"Every day," he conceded with a smile, as if it made him happy. "I never pray without naming her. I shall think of her until I die.

15

But I promised her that I would not trouble her. And neither will you."

Boston, New England, Spring 1685

Ned Ferryman stood on the jumble of quays and piers and wharves of Boston harbor, his collar turned against the cold wind, watching his barrels of herbs — dried sassafras, black cohosh roots, and ginseng leaves — roll down the stone quay and up the gangplank to the moored ship. Six barrels were already stowed belowdecks, and Ned squinted through the hatch to make sure that they were lashed tight and covered with an oilskin.

Beside him on the quayside the master of the ship laughed shortly. "Not to worry, Mr. Ferryman, they're safely aboard." He glanced down at Ned's worn leather satchel and the small sack of his goods. "Is this all you have for your cabin? No trunks?"

"That's all."

The cabin boy from the ship came running down the gangplank and scooped up the sack. Ned slung the satchel around his shoulder.

"You'll have heard the king's dead?" the captain asked. "I was the first ship to bring the news. I shouted it the moment we threw a line to shore. Who'd have thought a king that lived so wild would die in his own bed? God bless King Charles, lived a rogue and died a papist. His brother James will have

16

nipped on the throne by the time we get home."

"Only if they crown him," Ned remarked skeptically. "James the papist? And that papist wife alongside him?"

"Eh — I don't care for him myself — but what choice is there?"

"The Duke of Monmouth, the king's own son, a man who promises liberty, and freedom to choose your own religion."

"Born a bastard. And we can't send a Stuart king on his travels again. We've only just got them back."

A rare smile crossed Ned's stern face. "I don't see why they can't go again," he said. "What has any Stuart ever done for a workingman?"

"We'll know when we get there," the captain summed up. "We sail with the tide, just after midday. There's a noon gun."

"Aye, I know Boston," Ned said shortly.

"You've been here awhile?" The captain was curious about his quiet passenger, his deeply tanned skin, and his shock of gray hair. "It's a great city for making a fortune, isn't it?"

Ned shook his head. "I don't care for a fortune, stolen from natives who gave all they had at first. I make a small living, gathering herbs. But now it's time for me to go home. I'll be aboard before noon."

He turned from the quayside to go back to the inn to settle his slate. Coming from the opposite direction, tied in a line with tarry ropes, were a score of prisoners trailing their way to a ship for the plantations. Ned could tell at once that they were the people of several different Indian nations: the high topknots and shaven heads of some, and others had a sleek bob. Each face showed different tattoos: some high on the cheekbones or some marked straight across the forehead. There were even one or two wearing the proud all-black stain of "warpaint": the sign that a man was sworn to fight to the death. They were roped in a line, dressed in a muddle of ragged English clothes, shivering in the cold wind, alike in their shuffling pace — hobbled by tight ropes — and in the defeated stoop of their shoulders.

"Netop," Ned whispered in Pokanoket, as they went past him. *"Netop."*

Those who were closest heard the greeting — "friend" in their forbidden language — but they did not look up.

"Where they going?" Ned asked the red-faced man who was herding them, his hands in his pockets, a finely carved pipe clamped in the corner of his mouth.

"Sugar Islands." He turned his head and barked: "Wait!"

Obediently, the line shuddered to a halt.

"God help them," Ned said.

"He won't. They're all pagans."

Dourly, Ned turned away, spitting out the

18

bitter taste in his mouth, when he half heard a whisper, as quiet as a leaf falling in the forest:

"Nippe Sannup!"

He turned at the familiar sound of his name in Pokanoket: "Waterman."

"Who calls me?"

"Webe, pohquotwussinnan wutch matchitut."

A steady black gaze met Ned's. A youth, beardless and slight. There was no pleading in his face, but his lips formed the words: *"Nippe Sannup."*

"I need a boy, a servant," Ned lied. "I'm going to England. I need a lad to serve me on the ship."

"You don't have to buy one of these," the man advised him. "Just shout in the inn yard and half a dozen little white rats will pop up their heads, desperate to get home."

"No, I want a savage," Ned improvised rapidly. "I collect Indian herbs, and pagan carvings. Things like your pipe — that's savage work, isn't it? My goods'll sell better with a savage lad to carry them around. I'll buy one of 'em off you now," Ned said. He pointed to the youth. "That one."

"Oh, I couldn't let that one go," the man said at once. "He's going to grow like a weed, that one: thicken up, broaden out, going to be strong. I'll get good money for him."

"He won't last three seconds in the fields," Ned contradicted. "The voyage alone'll kill

19

him. There's nowt on him, and he's got that look in his eyes."

"They die just to disoblige me!" the jailer said irritably. "They don't take to slavery. Nobody'd buy one, if you could get an African. But a slave's a slave. You've got it for life — however long it lasts. What'll you give me?"

"Fifty dollars, Spanish dollars," Ned said, naming a price at random.

"Done," the man said so quickly that Ned knew it was too much. "Sure you want that one? Another pound buys you this one, he's bigger."

"No," Ned said. "I want a young one, easier to train."

"You hold the pistol while I untie him," the jailer said, pulling a pistol from his belt, showing it to the prisoners, who turned their heads away, as if in disdain. He pressed it into Ned's hands. "If anyone moves, shoot them in the foot: right?"

"Right," Ned said, taking the heavy firearm in his hand and pointing it at the huddled crowd.

The jailer took a knife out of his boot and slashed through the ropes on either side of the youth, pushing him, still tied and hobbled, towards Ned. He made the trailing ropes into two rough but serviceable loops and handed them to Ned, like the long reins for a young horse, as he took back his pistol.

20

Ned opened his satchel and counted out the coins. "Does he have any papers?"

The man laughed. "Do cows have papers?" he demanded. "Do pigs? Of course he don't. But we can take him to the blacksmith and brand him with your initial on his cheek."

Ned felt the cords in his hand tighten, as the slim youth braced himself against terror.

"No need," he said. "We sail in an hour. I'll load him on board now and lock him in my cabin."

"Mind he don't drown himself," the jailer said. "They do it the moment they get the chance. Someone told me they think they will rise out of the waves on a muskrat." He laughed loudly, showing his yellow stumps of teeth, rotted by sugar and rum.

"Yes, they do think that . . ." Ned remembered his friend telling him the Pequot legend of the making of the world: a muskrat bringing earth from the seabed as a gift of life from the animal to the first woman in the world.

"Take a brace?" the jailer gestured. "You can have another for the same price?"

"Nay." Ned tugged gently on the rope that trailed from the lad's tied wrists and led the way to the ship. The boy followed with his shuffling walk. Ned did not look back, no white man looks for his slave, and the boy hobbled behind him.

Ned did not speak to the lad, not even when they were on board. He locked him in the windowless cabin and found the load-master and paid for another passage, a quarter price as it was a slave. He refused the offer to chain the boy in the cargo hold and pay for him as if he were baggage. He went back to the inn and bought a few shirts and a pair of breeches for the lad, and then he stayed on deck until the captain shouted, the gangway was drawn in, the ropes cast off and the bell towers and roofs of the city got smaller and smaller until the new city of Boston was just a smudge on the horizon, the sun sinking behind it. Ned stretched his aching back and went through the hatch and down the ladder to the tiny cabins below the deck.

The lad was seated on the floor, his head resting on his knees, as if he did not dare to touch the narrow bunk. When the door opened on Ned, carrying a gimbaled candle-stick in one hand, the bundle of clothes in the other, he rose to his feet, alert as a cornered deer. His breath came a little quicker, but he showed no sign of fear. Ned, knowing the extraordinary courage of the Po-kanoket, was not surprised. He put down the candle, the counterweight base moving gently with the ship to hold the candle upright.

"You know me," Ned fumbled to remember the words of the banned language of Poka-noket. "You called me *Nippe Sannup*."

The youth nodded stiffly.

22

"Have you seen me in the wilderness? Have I traded with your people?"

The boy said nothing.

"Have your people traded furs with me? Or gathered herbs for me?"

Still there was no answer.

"What language do you speak?" Ned asked in the forbidden language of the Pokanoket, then he tried again in Mohawk.

"I can speak English," the youth said slowly.

"What is your people?" Ned demanded.

The boy's face was expressionless, but one tear rose up and rolled down his face. He did not brush it aside, as if the name that might never be spoken was Sorrow. "We are forbidden to say our name," he said quietly. "I knew you when I was a child. You were *Nippe Sannup,* the ferryman at Hadley. My people took your ferry when the Quinnehtukqut was in flood."

Ned felt the familiar sense of longing for that lost time. "Fifteen years ago? When I kept the ferry at Hadley?"

The youth nodded.

"That was a lifetime. You must've been a child."

"Are we at sea? Is the boat at sea?" he suddenly demanded.

"Aye."

"You will not throw me over the side?"

"Why would I do that, fool? I just rescued you! And paid a fortune!"

23

"You have saved me from the plantations?"

"Aye, we're going to London."

The youth gritted his teeth on the terror of another unknown destination. "I thank you."

Ned grinned. "You don't look too thankful."

"I am. You knew my grandmother, her name was Quiet Squirrel. D'you remember her? She made your snowshoes. D'you remember them? And my mother?"

"Quiet Squirrel!" Ned exclaimed. "She did! She did make my snowshoes. And she taught me . . . She taught me every —" He broke off. "Is she . . ."

"She's gone to the dawn," the boy said simply. "All my people are gone. All my family are dead. Just a few of us were captured alive. The village is gone. You can't even see the postholes. They burned us out and they plowed our ground. They have made us . . ." He sought for the word. ". . . invisible."

Ned sat down heavily on the side of the bunk. "Invisible? How can a people become invisible?" He had a sudden, vivid memory of the village of Norwottuck: the houses around the central fire, the children playing, the women grinding corn, the men dragging in a shot deer, the girls carrying long spears loaded with fresh fish. Impossible to think it was all gone, yet he knew it was impossible that it had survived the three years of bitter warfare. "And you . . ." He looked at the

24

youth. "Were you one of the little lads?"

The youth pressed his lips together as if he would hold in dangerous words, but he forced himself to speak. "I met you when I was a child of six summers. You used to make me laugh when we crossed the river on your ferry. Back then, I was called Red Berries in Rain."

Ned's eyes widened; he got to his feet, put his hand under the youth's chin, turned his face to the light of the candle. "Red Berries in Rain?" he whispered.

There was a day in his mind, long ago, more than fifteen years ago, when the women had been on his ferry, and they had been laughing at the little girl who had hidden behind her grandmother and peeped up at him with huge dark eyes. "You're a lass?" he asked, disbelieving. "You're that little lass?"

She nodded. "Please . . . Please don't give me to the sailors," she whispered.

"God's blood! D'you think I am a beast?"

She flinched from his outrage. "The jailer gave my sister to the sailors."

"I'd never do such a thing!" he swore. "I'd never — well, you're not to know. But I have a sister in England! I have a niece! God knows, I'd never . . ."

"I said I was a boy, and they gave me a shirt and breeches."

"Aye, it's best." Ned gestured to the patched breeches and old shirts on the bunk.

"You'd better stay as a lad till we get to England. We'll say you're my serving boy."

"Thank you," she said. "I don't want to be a girl until I am a girl of the Dawnlands again."

"What'll we call you?" he asked. "I can't call you Red Berries in Rain."

"It was a mosmezi tree," she offered. "You had one growing by your gate. A slight tree with white flowers in spring, and in autumn: red berries? We use the bark for healing?"

"I remember," he said. But he did not want the pain of remembering the tree at his gate, and the ferry across the river, and the women who had been his friends, and who had walked with him into the New England village, sure of their welcome, with baskets of food and fish on strings. "It's a rowan tree," he told her. "We can call you Rowan. And here . . ." He pushed the clothes towards her. "You'd better get out of those rags, they're probably lousy. I'll get the galley to boil them."

"Can I wash?" she asked.

He hesitated, knowing that at every dawn, her people would wash and pray, facing the rising sun. They were the People of the Dawnlands, they were the people of the long dark coast that was the first to see the sun every day. Of all the unknown peoples in all the great forests that stretched to the west far away behind them, they were the first to see the first light.

"Not like you do at dawn," he told her. "But I can get you a jug of water and some soap." He put his hand on the latch of the door.

"Shouldn't I get it?" she asked him. "As I am your slave? You're not mine."

She surprised him into a laugh. "Aye, I'm not. Come then, I'll show you the way to the galley and the stores, and around the ship. You should really sleep in the hold, but you'll be safer in my cabin. You can have the bunk, I'll take the floor."

"No! No!" she refused at once. "I sleep on the floor." She looked up at him to see if he would smile again. "I am your slave. You're not mine."

"I'd never have a slave," he told her. "All my life I have believed that men — even women — should be free. I'm going back to England now to help set my countrymen free."

She nodded, following the rapid words and watching his lips, so she saw his smile when it came. "But you can sleep on the floor."

"Because you have a niece?" she asked him with a gleam in her dark eyes.

"Because I am old enough to be your grandfather," he said dourly. "And as stiff in the morning as frozen laundry on a washing line."

27

Ned had guessed she would wake before dawn, and he was instantly aware of her, awake but silent. "You'll want to see sunrise," he said quietly into the pitch-darkness.

"Can I?"

Outside Ned's door a ladder led upwards to a battened-down hatch. Ned went first, lifted the hatch, and breathed the cold saltiness of the sea air. He put the cover aside, climbed out, and turned to help her, but she was already up on deck gulping in the clean breeze, her arms thrown wide as if she would have the wind blow through her clothes, blow defeat out of her soul.

The sky was lightening all around them, but the sun was not yet up. Ned raised his hand in acknowledgment to the steersman and led the way fore so that they were facing east, facing England. There was a clean bucket on a frosty rope for sluicing down the deck. Ned lowered it into the sea and felt it tug in his hands. He hauled it back in and put it at her feet. "Best I can do," he said, and stepped back.

Rowan looked out along the bowsprit to where the horizon gleamed with a cold pale light. She loosened the shirt at her neck; she did not dare stand naked as the ritual demanded, but she splayed her bare toes on the

28

deck and stood tall, swaying slightly at the roll and dip of the ship through the waters. She took a cupped handful of icy water and poured it over her head, over her neck, another full into the face. She tasted the salt and opened her eyes. She whispered: "Great Spirit, Mother Earth, Grandmother Moon, Grandfather Sun, I thank you. I pray to the four directions . . ."

Carefully she turned to the four points of the compass, looking out over gray rolling waves east then north, south, and west until she was facing the brighter horizon once more. "I thank you for all my relations: the winged nation, the creeping and crawling nation, the four-legged nation, the green and growing nation, and all things living in the water. Honoring the clans: the deer — *ahtuk,* the bear — *mosq,* the wolf — *mukquoshim,* the turtle — *tunnuppasog,* the snipe — *sasasō. Keihtanit taubot neanawayean.*"

The head of a silvery sun was rising from the gray faraway waters as she murmured the prayer. She bowed her head and poured more water over her head, her face, her neck, her breast, as the sun rose. She looked towards it, as if it might tell her how she should survive this extraordinary transition in her life, from one world to another, from one life to another, from one country to another. She had no fear. She felt the strength in her feet on the scrubbed wooden deck, the powerful beating of her heart, and the limitless confidence of youth.

St. James's Palace, London, Spring 1685

If Livia was nervous, as the Avery carriage drove through the rolling deer park and turned into the great arched doorway, she showed no sign. As the coach rattled through the imposing north gatehouse, the wheels echoing loudly on the cobbles, guardsmen saluting the Avery crest on the carriage door, Livia settled her cape around her, tied the silk ribbons on her hat, and straightened the ribbon bows over her shoulders. All she could see were the tall walls of red brick relieved with white pillars and mullioned windows. The carriage halted and the steps were let down. Livia's grip was firm on the footman's arm, her step light on the pavement. The lace edging on her hat did not tremble, the smile on her beautiful face was steady. Her tight bodice hid her breathlessness; the thick silk of her gown and her billowing petticoats swished around her as she followed the new queen's chief secretary into the first court, across the rigidly formal garden, through inner doors and up the stairs. Finally, the chief secretary nodded to two men-at-arms to throw open the double doors of the queen's presence chamber and announced: "Lady Livia Avery, Your Majesty."

The dark-haired queen was seated at the

window, looking far younger than her twenty-six years, some fine embroidery in an ivory frame beside her, two maids of honor sorting embroidery silks on low stools beside her and two ladies-in-waiting opposite her. In the corner of the room a lutist and a singer created a gentle warble, enough to mask indiscreet conversations from the hearing of the servants who stood at the buffet of silverware. Queen Mary Beatrice was wearing a deep-red silk gown trimmed with silver lace, cut very low over her breasts and across her arms to show her white shoulders. Her slim neck was loaded with jeweled necklaces, she had diamonds in her ears and chains of diamonds wrapped around her arms. Her dark hair was piled on her head, falling in ringlets to her shoulders. She turned a pale face to the door, but as she saw Livia she lit up. "Oh! Livia! My dearest Livia!" she exclaimed at once in Italian. "You have come! In this terrible weather! You have come to bring the spring!"

Livia sank into a deep curtsey and kept her head down, but the queen raised her at once and fell into her arms. She was slight — beneath the flowing embroidered silks Livia could feel a body as slim as a girl's. Over her shoulder Livia could see the grim faces of the other attendants as they noted the arrival of a new favorite.

"*Carissima,*" the queen whispered. "I have longed for you. I will be grateful for all my

31

life that you have come to me." She turned. "Are Lady Avery's rooms prepared for her?" she asked. "The best rooms, near mine."

Lady Isabella Wentworth rose up and dropped a small curtsey to Livia. "Shall I show Lady Avery to her rooms?"

"No!" The queen turned impulsively. "I'll come myself." She paused for a moment, shaken by a cough. "You all stay here," she said, catching her breath. Defying protocol, she took Livia's hand and the two of them followed Lady Wentworth from the presence chamber, through the privy chamber, through the queen's bedchamber to a gallery of doors for the ladies-in-waiting. One was already painted with the Avery crest. Livia's dark eyelashes hid the gleam in her eyes at the triumph, but she said nothing and waited for the footman to dart forward and swing open the door. Lady Wentworth stepped back to allow her queen and Livia to enter first.

Livia's drawing room had a warm fire in the grate, a pair of silk upholstered chairs before it, an expensive rug on the floor. There was a grand mahogany table with six dining chairs under the window so that she could dine with friends and enjoy the view of the privy gardens and beyond them the rolling lawns of the deer park. There were portraits on the walls and a tapestry depicting a white hart being brought down by huntsmen. There were sconces with candles and candelabra on the tables holding pure white wax candles. Livia crossed the room and looked out of the window. She allowed herself to imagine the south bank of the river, far away, due east. The poor wharf, the cargo ships bobbing in dirty water, the little home where she had gladly left her son so that she could rise, unhampered, to this greatness. She was pleased she could not see it — it was too far away — around the broad loop in the river, beyond London Bridge, beyond the Tower, far from the wealth and elegance of the royal palaces, far away from her new life.

"Is it all right?" the queen asked humbly.

Livia turned. "It's quite all right," she said, smiling. "It's perfect for me."

Reekie Wharf, London, Spring 1685

Beyond Livia's horizon, three and a half miles downriver, on the south bank, Ned stood for a moment to look at the Thames in flow, the waters rushing past the quay, the boats riding high, unladen, in the center of the stream.

On the distant opposite bank Ned could see the river wall was being extended, the mud and pebbles of the foreshore enclosed by great beams packed with stone. The green weeds and water had dried out, the wading birds had deserted it. New buildings, streets, slums, hovels were being built on a tumble of stone and rubble. The city was spreading downriver, making more and more wharves for more and more ships, as if trade itself were a new king who could demand selfish changes to England.

Rowan, close behind him, was dressed as a manservant: shoes and woolen stockings on her feet, wool breeches and a linen shirt and wool jacket under a warm traveling cape. A cap pulled low over her cropped dark hair completed the disguise. Ned led the way down the alley that ran between the warehouse and its neighbor, until he came to a lantern door set into the big wagon gates, which were bolted and closed for the night. Inside the yard, he could hear someone bedding down horses, the splash of water being pumped into a bucket, and the bang of the stable door. He put his hand on the iron ring to open the little door, but she saw him hesitate.

"I can hardly go in. I've not seen my sister for twenty-five years. I never thought I'd come back."

He turned the handle, opened the door, and stepped through. It was a prosperous yard, swept clean around raised beds of herbs. There were four big horses nodding over the stable doors, and two carts stored in the cart shed. The double doors that led to the warehouse were safely locked, but the door to the kitchen was half-open. Ned could see the cook bending over a new cast-iron stove. She turned as she heard the lantern gate and came to look over the bolted lower door, wiping her hands on her apron.

"Is it a load?"

"No," said Ned. "I've come to see Mrs. Reekie."

"If you want the herbs, I can sell them."

"I'm her brother, come home from New England. I'm Ned Ferryman."

"Oh, my Lord!" she exclaimed and then clapped her hand to her mouth to stifle the oath. "Oh, my word! Well! You're very welcome, sir. Come in! Come in! You should have come to the front door, not in the yard like a carter. Come in, and I'll tell them you're here."

She swung open the bottom half of the door and shouted to the kitchen maid to come and take their bags. She went surging into the hall, to the parlor at the front of the house, which overlooked the quay and the river. "You'll never guess who's in the yard!" she exclaimed to the middle-aged couple in the room. "You'll never guess."

The woman rose to her feet. "Of course I won't guess," she said, a tolerant smile on her face. "Who's come at this time of night to the yard gate, Tabs?"

"Your uncle Ned!" the cook exclaimed triumphantly. "Who would ever've guessed that! Your uncle Ned from the Americas. Large as life and his lad at his side."

Alys went swiftly past her to the kitchen

35

and then checked as she saw the broad gray-haired man, swinging his satchel to the floor, and behind him, the most beautiful boy she had ever seen, dark-haired, dark-eyed, head up, light on his feet as a deer.

"Uncle Ned?" Alys asked uncertainly. "Tabs said you were my uncle Ned?" and when he looked up and smiled at her, she said with sudden certainty: "It *is* you!"

Alys's husband, Captain Shore, filled the doorway to the hall. "Ned Ferryman?" he queried.

Alys was in Ned's arms, hugging him, patting him, pulling back to look into his worn, grooved face. "Uncle Ned, God bless you! We never thought to see you again!"

"I know. I never thought I'd come back. But here I am!"

"Praise God you're safe, after such travels!"

"Amen, amen. My sister Alinor is well?" He looked around for her.

"Yes — speaking of you only last night. And you know there's a new king on the throne? Crowned and anointed just last week? King James. Does that mean you're safe to come home now? And the troubles are all forgotten?"

"They're not all forgotten," he said steadily.

"You've not come back to rise up again? You're not for the Protestant duke?" she demanded anxiously, interrogating his face with a frowning gaze.

"Hush," Captain Shore intervened. "Come into the parlor, sir. I take it you're my uncle-in-law, and I am your nephew Abel Shore."

"Congratulations, and I'm glad to meet you at last!" Ned said. "I sent you some buckskins for your marriage bed."

"I sleep under them every night," the Captain said. "Coziest bedding I've ever had. Much needed this winter gone. We're grateful. And who's this?"

"My lad. This is my serving boy: Rowan."

"Well, come in, both of you," Captain Shore said. "Have you dined?"

"There's enough for us all," Alys assured him. "The maid can run out to the bakehouse and get a chicken pie. Uncle Ned, I must take you upstairs to Ma at once. You know, she was speaking of you only last night. She dreamed of you, at sea on dark tides."

"Aye, I wondered if she'd know I was on deep waters," he said. "But you'd better prepare her."

"We'll wait for you down here," Captain Shore said, waving Rowan back to the kitchen. "You get warm in the kitchen, lad. And, Uncle Ned, if Mrs. Reekie wants you to dine upstairs with her, sir, you just say the word. Sometimes she comes down for dinner, sometimes she don't. It's always her wish, just as she wants."

Ned followed his niece up the wooden stairs to the next floor. To his right was the door to his sister's room, and to his left the bedroom that Alys shared with her husband, and another door to the smaller spare room. The narrow stairs for the servants' rooms went up into the eaves of the roof.

Alys tapped on the door and went in, leaving it half-open. "Ma," Ned heard her say. "Be steady, Ma. I have some news."

"I can tell it's good news from your face," he heard his sister reply.

At the sound of her voice he could not make himself wait any longer. He pushed open the door. "It's me, Alinor. I'm come home."

Alinor rose up from the sofa, her pale face flushed with joy, her hands outstretched to him. "Ah, Ned! You've come home at last." And in a moment, she was folded in his arms.

Later that night, after a bustle of preparation and dinner and drinking of healths and exchanging news, Ned went to Alinor's room to say good night and sat on the end of the sofa. "I daren't keep you late," he said. "Alys gave me such a scowl. Are you tired?"

She put her hand to her chest where her breath came short. "I'm too happy to be tired. I always thought I'd see you in this life again, Ned. But I never dreamed you'd come home like a merman out of water, without a word of warning."

"I never thought I'd sit at a table with my

family again. I've been solitary for so long."

"But now you've got Rowan for company?"

"He's just with me for the voyage," he said. "I can't bear to keep a servant, Sister. You know my feelings. I paid for his passage over, but he's free."

She slid a sideways look at him. "Rowan? Named for a tree? Neither girl nor boy but a being from the forest?"

He smiled ruefully. "Of course, you saw her at once. Aye, she's a lass. The granddaughter of a woman who was kind to me when I was first in New England. They call themselves the Pokanoket, the People of the Dawnlands." He corrected himself. "No. Not anymore. They did. They were the ones killed in the wars, and now their name is forbidden."

"Have you escaped one war to wage another?" she asked him acutely.

He glanced to her closed bedroom door, as if even in her own house, he was wary of eavesdroppers. "Aye, I got a message," he said shortly. "Old comrades tell me that the new king is a papist and a French spy. They say that no one will stand for it, the people will rise again and put the Duke of Monmouth in as a new Lord Protector. Another Cromwell. So I came at once. Like an old horse at the sound of the trumpets! To see it happen — the freeing of the people. Once again."

She nodded. "It's true," she said. "Captain Shore keeps his own counsel, and we're far away from St. James's Palace, but even the merchants' coffeehouses say that the new king prays like a papist in a foreign tongue, kneels for Mass with his foreign wife, and the court is bought and sold by France. There's not an honest man among them. And the young Duke of Monmouth is said to be in the Low Countries, building a fleet. They say he'll come to save us and the Church of England. The country'll be divided again into royalist against roundhead."

"There'll be a war?" he confirmed. "Another civil war?"

"Not for you," she urged. "Not for you, who left England rather than be subject to a king. You've done enough, Brother. Come to watch if you must. But don't you risk a beating. You can't bear that grief again."

His slow smile told her that he regretted nothing. "Nay," he said. "All my life I've thought that God made man and woman, not kings and servants. I was proud to serve under Cromwell to set the men of England free. I was glad we won our freedom. I was sorry we gave it away again. I'd be proud to fight for the men of England once again."

"We can't," she told him. "The family can't. We've taken years to build the warehouse trade, and now we have our own ship: Captain Shore's ship. We've bought the wharf next door, we trade in fine things from Sarah in Venice. Johnnie is a writer at the East India

40

Company and Rob is a doctor, he's put up his door knocker in the City — our Rob! A proper doctor! We can't throw that away for the king's bastard. We can't do it, Ned. You can't ask it of us — not of the young ones when they're doing so well. Not of Captain Shore and Alys now they're settled."

"No, no," Ned said quickly, clasping her hand. "Not any one of you. I'll go to Monmouth as a single man, without ties, without family. This is my battle — not theirs. If the Duke of Monmouth takes me into his service, I'll be Ned Ferryman come from New England to serve my countrymen — and nothing to link the Reekie wharf to me."

"You'll think me chickenhearted," she said ruefully.

He shook his head. "I wouldn't have you lose your home again. Once was enough."

"It's not home," she said quietly, thinking of their house beside their ferry on the tidelands. "But it's a good living."

"Course," he agreed. "And maybe I'll come out of this so well that I'll buy you a house at Foulmire, and you and I will end our days there, watching the waters rise and fall in the harbor, with no lord ruling over us and no king over England, and it'll be a new dawn."

St. James's Palace, London, Spring 1685
The newly crowned queen was sick: bleached
by the pain in her chest, in her back, cold
despite the heaped lambswool covers on her
bed. No doctor had been able to cure the
cough which came and went with the seasons;
the hard-hearted courtiers said it was a weakness of her family, and that she would die
before she was thirty. She would see no one
but Livia, who lay with her in the bed, as
close as a lover, warming her with the heat of
her body.

Mary Beatrice could not rest. She spoke
feverishly of the conversion of England, of
the winning of all the souls to the true faith,
with fire if need be. She coughed and said
that she must have a son, a son baptized into
the Roman Catholic church to cement the
conversion, that her life would be wasted if
she died of this cough, of weakness, before
giving the Holy Father a papist prince of
Wales, an heir of the true faith for England.

Livia, too much of a courtier to argue, thought the country had been Protestant for too long to change back again, the church lands sucked into private estates, the abbeys rebuilt as private houses, the nuns married off, the priests vanished. Not even the stones stood where the monks had set them, the relics of the saints were missing from honored tombs, the pilgrim ways growing grass. The lands dedicated to holiness were growing wheat at a profit. English lords had exchanged God for great wealth, and it would be hard to change them back again.

"My son will be crowned by the Pope," the queen predicted. "Not like us, in secret."

"You were crowned by the Archbishop of Canterbury in Westminster Abbey, before everyone?" Livia corrected her gently, thinking she must be delirious.

"Of course, we had to go to Westminster Abbey, as the Protestants wanted, but it was an empty show. We were first crowned and anointed in secret, in the Roman Catholic chapel at Whitehall, by the king's confessor."

Livia was aghast. "My dear, you must never repeat that! People would go mad if they found out. They would tear down the palace."

"Of course, it is secret," the queen said more calmly. "But think of the glory! I am the first queen crowned in the true church since England turned heretic. Think of that! I am the first queen crowned by a priest since the sainted Catherine of Aragon, since Queen Mary."

"Because the church changed! England has changed."

"I will change it back . . ." Her voice trailed off as she fell asleep, but Livia did not close her eyes. She gazed up at the rich canopy, half dreaming, half planning, as if she could see the future in the golden embroidered sunburst, the circling stars of silver thread, trying to imagine if this queen and king could dominate the country, could remake England. Mary Beatrice stirred in her sleep, and Livia turned to her like a lover and kissed the line of her neck from her ear to her collarbone, pressing herself gently, tightening her hold.

Reekie Wharf, London, Spring 1685
Ned, flushed and awkward, waiting for his nephew, Rob, and the family's foster son, Matthew, to arrive for dinner, felt too big for the parlor at the front of the warehouse, ungainly at the window overlooking the river, awkward at the dining table. In the kitchen, Rowan, equally out of place, was clumsily loading a tray with a bottle of wine and glasses and an earthenware pitcher of small ale.

"Take it! Take it!" Tabs commanded, sweating over the stove. "You're his serving lad, ain't you? Serve it!"

Rowan abandoned the attempt to claim that

she was a serving lad who did not serve, and carried the heavy tray into the parlor.

"Here, lad! Put it down before you drop it," Ned said, helping her with the heavy tray as the glasses clinked dangerously together. "Neither of us is at ease here."

Alinor, seated at the fireside, smiled at Rowan. "I hope you'll feel at home soon."

There was a knock at the front door.

"That'll be Matthew, home from college," Alys said, emerging from the countinghouse at the back of the hall, her husband, Captain Shore, behind her. "Or maybe my brother, Rob, come early."

Ned nodded to Rowan. "Answer it, lad."

"How?" she said, very low.

"Just open the door and stand back and bow. Don't be a gowk."

Rowan threw him an exasperated look, but went to the door and opened it to a tall, slim man aged about fifty years. He handed her his fringed hat and cape without remark and went past her into the parlor. Rowan went to shut the front door when she heard a shout from the quayside — "Hold up!"

She hesitated, as a long-legged youth of about fifteen came bounding towards the open door, light-footed over the cobbles.

"Here — you're new!" he exclaimed. "Did you come with my great-uncle Ned? From America?"

She nodded as he slipped past her and into

45

the parlor of his home. The door closed on them, and she scowled at her pang of self-pity. It was strange to think that a man who had always appeared so solitary, in his lonely house, beside a cold river in the Dawnlands, should have had all this behind him: family, house, business, on the side of the great river of London; and that she — a girl embedded in her family, born of ancestors from the dawn of time, whose seat was the cliffs of Montaup — should find herself all alone in a strange flat land that faced north.

In the parlor, Ned was greeting Rob after a gap of twenty-five years. "A doctor's knocker on your door, half of London coming to you for physic, and a wife and child! I'm so glad for you. It's more than we dreamed of, that first day when we sent you to be apprenticed at Chichester. And your ma in tears at losing her little boy!"

"I remember you giving me money for dinner, in case they underfed me! You got me started, Uncle Ned, and then I was lucky in Padua at my university and then in my practice in Venice," Rob told his uncle.

"Thank God you got out of there safely."

"Ah, it was a long time ago, and we don't speak of it." Rob glanced towards the fostered boy, Matthew. "Better for the lad that we don't."

"Secrets?" Ned's grizzled brows twitched together in a frown.

46

"Some things are better left unsaid," Rob said firmly.

"A lad should know his father's name."

"Only his mother knows that!" Rob said low, with a half smile. "Livia Avery left us far behind when she married Sir James. She left her son for my ma and sister to raise as their own, without a backward glance. We don't speak of her, and he never asks. But I should say — my wife, Julia, sends her apologies. She hopes to visit tomorrow."

"For sure," Ned said easily. He glanced back at Matthew, who was watching the two of them. "But what name does the lad go by? Not yours?"

"Not mine! Before she married for name and a title, Livia called herself Picci, sometimes da Picci, and Matthew uses that." He glanced over at Matthew. "I'm telling my uncle Ned you're doing well in your studies."

"I'm working hard, whatever Ma Alys suspects!" the youth assured them. "I'm lucky to have a place at Lincoln's Inn."

Alys offered him a glass of wine and water. "He had to do a speech in Latin! Can you imagine?"

"Good for you, lad." Ned offered a callused hand. "Think of us having a lawyer in the family!"

Susie the maid put her head in the room. "Am I to serve dinner now?"

"Yes," Captain Shore told her. "We won't

wait for Johnnie."

Everyone drew up their chairs to the table as the cook, Tabs; the maid, Susie; and Rowan brought dish after dish, some of them bought from the bakehouse, some of them cooked at the stove, the butter cold from the larder, the small ale brewed in the malthouse across the yard.

They heard the front door, and Alys's son, Johnnie, came into the parlor, his hat in his hand, his brown hair ruffled by the wind from crossing the river from the City. "Grandmother Alinor, Ma, I'm sorry I'm late. I had a ship come in with mail, and I couldn't leave before I read it." His brown gaze fell on his great-uncle. "And you must be my uncle Ned! Sir! Welcome home!"

Ned stood and hugged the handsome young man. "Look at you! I left a lad of eleven years, and now you're a man of business."

Johnnie thrust his thumbs in his waistcoat and spun around to show his great-uncle his fine embroidered jacket and his deep crimson breeches. He had his mother's golden brown hair and square, honest face. Ned laughed at his vanity and clapped him on the shoulder as he sat down at the dinner table.

"He always wanted to work for the East India Company," Alys said proudly, passing her son, Johnnie, a plate. "And he trades on his own account."

48

"Do you?" asked Ned. "What sort of goods?"

"Mostly silk and dry goods," Johnnie said, helping himself to a slice of pie. "I get opium for Uncle Rob, spices for Ma to sell to grocers. And I send silk from India: overland — to my sister, Sarah, in Venice — and by sea — to here." He looked up, as Rowan awkwardly held a dish. "Hello, who's this?"

She did not bow and lower her eyes as a trained servant would have done. She did not wait for her owner to answer for her like a slave. She met his gaze like an equal. "I am Rowan. I came with your uncle Ned."

"A slave?" He turned to Ned.

"Certainly not."

"I choose to serve him," Rowan told Johnnie.

"You make it sound like he's honored!" He smiled at her.

"He is not honored," Rowan corrected gravely. "And I am no slave. We have an agreement."

"A native Leveller," Rob observed quietly to his mother, Alinor. "I think Uncle Ned has met his match."

"And are we equals?" Johnnie asked Rowan, smiling. "All equals? My great-uncle Ned, whom you agree to serve; my uncle Rob, a physician; and my ma and grandmother, who own this wharf; and Captain Shore, who owns the ship at the quay outside? Do you

49

have no betters?"

Rowan glanced at Alinor to see if she might answer, and at her nod, she quietly replied: "Sir, I am very sure you are a great family. But I was born one of the People. And we are the first to see the sun in the morning."

"How very Copernican!" Rob was amused by this exchange.

"D'you even know where the sun rises?" Rowan challenged Johnnie.

He hesitated. "There, isn't it?" Johnnie pointed to his right.

"Isn't that north?" Rob asked.

"It's downriver," Alys told her son. "Fancy you not knowing!"

Captain Shore laughed. "Just as well for you all that I know!"

Alinor pointed due east.

"It is that way," Rowan agreed.

"But it doesn't matter to us," Johnnie pointed out. "We go by addresses in London, the names of streets, we don't navigate by the sky."

"I don't know your streets," she admitted. "But I know where I am under the sky. And if your streets tumble down . . ."

"Some of them were burned to nothing," Alinor pointed out.

"Then there is only the sky. And you will not know where you are. But I always will." She took the empty dish from Johnnie and went back to the kitchen as Ned gave a little

50

crow of laughter.

"You think you're having an ordinary talk, and suddenly you're on to the stars, or the words of the wind."

"What're you going to do with him, though?" Rob asked, as Susie followed Rowan out of the room. "Clearly, he can't serve."

Alinor and Ned, brother and sister, exchanged a hidden smile at her son. "Ah, Rob, how can you be such a great physician and yet blind?" Alinor asked him. "D'you not see that's a girl?"

"A girl? A native girl?" Alys exclaimed. "I didn't know!"

"Bless me!" Captain Shore said.

"But why's she dressed like that?" Johnnie demanded.

"It was easier that she pass as a boy while we were traveling," Ned said. "And now I have to find somewhere that she can be safe as a girl, and work that she can do as a maid. I can't take a girl where I am going."

"Where are you going, Uncle Ned?" Rob asked.

"Better that I don't speak of it here."

Johnnie was alert to the danger. "You're not expecting trouble, sir?"

Ned shook his head and said nothing. Rob spoke into the silence: "Uncle, you've been away too long. It's not the same cause, it's not the same Stuart. Your man Cromwell is dead and buried. The Charles they invited

51

back is dead too, and when his royal brother James took the crown, they shouted Vivat Rex for him! Nobody likes the king's religion, not many like him. But the country has chosen him. There'll not be another civil war."

"Maybe not," Ned said briefly.

Matthew looked curiously from one determined face to another.

"I promise you," Rob told his uncle, "the war you fought is over, there will not be another."

"Better that I don't speak of it."

St. James's Palace, London, Spring 1685
Mary Beatrice was half carried home from the state opening of parliament. Livia received her in her arms at the doorway of her privy chamber, helped her into her chair, taking the crown from her head and passing it aside as if it were nothing in her haste to get the heavy robes off the queen's shoulders.

"It was too much for you," she scolded. "I said you should not have gone."

Mary Beatrice shook her head, sipping wine and water. "It wasn't the weight of the crown — that was nothing — it was what they said!" she exclaimed. "What he said!"

"Why? What did they say? What did they dare to say?"

Mary Beatrice pulled Livia close so she could whisper. "It was the king himself! He said the most dreadful thing. He told them

— we are going to be invaded!"

Livia was stunned. "Invaded?"

"The Earl of Argyll — a most desperate rebel — has ships and men, allied with the Duke of Monmouth, the late king's son, and they have sworn to overthrow us!"

Livia gave a little gasp. "What?"

"So the king told the parliament. Argyll can call up every Scot in the land. He's the chief of the Campbells, and there are thousands of them. He's a bitter Presbyterian — so all the heretics will follow him. And everyone in England loves Monmouth, they wanted the late king to make him legitimate, name him heir instead of us. And now, he and the earl have joined together and landed somewhere in Scotland. They'll march on London. They'll muster thousands."

"But why would the king announce it?" Livia demanded. "Why tell everyone? Won't they all run to them?"

"He thought he was being clever," she said uncertainly. "He thought to outwit parliament into giving him everything he wants: the money to raise an army, the right to call out the militia. Parliament are so wicked as to not trust kings: they never allow royal troops. But my husband has triumphed. He has frightened them into giving him new powers. More money to raise his own army. He says it's a victory for us? He says it's a victory for all kings." She looked doubtfully

53

at Livia.

"Well, yes, if his new army can beat the earl and the Duke of Monmouth."

"Not together! No one could beat them together!" The queen turned from the watching court, whispered that she would go to her bedroom. Livia nodded to the footman to open the doors, carry the queen into her bedroom, and close the door on the anxious faces.

"You must be calm," Livia urged, kneeling before the queen to chafe her hands, heavy with rings. "You have to be as still as a field for sowing. A son will make us all safe."

"It's too late for my baby if Argyll and James of Monmouth march on London. Nothing will save us if the people flock to Monmouth! He was commander of the English army, and they all loved him . . . even I loved him, we all did . . . He was the most handsome young man, the most charming, the king's most beloved son . . ."

"No, no . . ."

"And he has a son of his own — a son to be heir to our throne. He has two, he has three! God has blessed him with . . . I don't know how many heirs! Protestant heirs. Perhaps God will give him the throne as well!"

"No! No!" Livia felt more and more helpless against the rising distress of the young queen, overwhelmed by her rapid speech, catching her sense of panic. "No! You know you are chosen by God to bring the faith to England. The Pope himself sent you. You've only been queen for a month! God would not —"

"Maybe that's all I'll ever be! Queen of four weeks! Only four weeks and already there's an army marching on us. They don't want us! They hate me!"

"No, they don't," Livia said staunchly, completely out of her depth. "And anyway, who cares what the people want?"

Reekie Wharf, London, Spring 1685
Rob reluctantly brought his wife to meet his uncle Ned, knowing that she would dislike him on sight as a workingman, and an exiled Cromwell soldier, and that Ned would dismiss her as an idle woman of fashion.

Alinor watched from her high bedroom window, as the wherry carrying Rob and Julia bobbed at the Horsleydown water stairs, and then she crossed her room and called down the stairs. "Susie, open the front door. The doctor and Mrs. Reekie are here."

Instead of Susie, she saw Rowan's dark crown and then her smile as she looked upwards through the well of the stairs. "Susie's out in the yard. Shall I open the door?"

"Lord, no." Alinor laughed. "Mrs. Julia would take a fit. Send Tabs, and you keep out of her way."

Rowan nodded and called Tabs, who surged out, wiping her hands on her apron.

"Hello, Tabs," Rob said, as his wife flinched at the cook opening the front door. "We've come to see my ma."

"Upstairs," Tabs said shortly, heading back to the kitchen. "And Mrs. Shore is in the countinghouse," she called over her shoulder.

"Oh, I want to see Alys," Rob remarked and turned into the warehouse, ignoring his wife's touch on his arm.

Julia mounted the stairs slowly, braced herself before the closed door to Alinor's bedroom, tapped on the panel with one gloved hand, and entered. "Mother Alinor," she said faintly, brushing a kiss on Alinor's cheek and sinking down on the sofa.

"Dear Julia," Alinor replied. "How are you today? I'm sorry you weren't well enough to come yesterday."

"It's my head." Julia loosened the ribbons and took off her hat, as if the weight of feathers was too much for her.

"I should give you a tisane." Alinor gestured at the muslin bags that were spread over the table before her chair, as she sewed them for herbs for tea.

"Rob gives me laudanum." Julia averted her eyes from evidence of Alinor's work. "It's the only thing that helps me."

"Surely not every day?"

"Without it, I can do nothing." She smiled, as if it were an achievement.

"I have to be doing something."

"I wasn't raised to it," Julia said flatly.

Alinor nodded, gritting her teeth on a retort. "I know that, my dear," she said. "How is Hester? I am sorry you didn't bring her. I haven't seen her for a long time."

"If only Rob would set up a proper carriage . . ." Julia's soft complaint died away. Her daughter, Hester, wore a metal brace on her left leg to straighten her club foot, and Julia had established early on that she could not allow the child to cross the river on a wherry boat. She had asked Rob to set up a carriage on her wedding day, and plaintively repeated her request every month of every one of the fourteen years, ever since.

"Well, I shall have to visit you," Alinor said cheerfully, avoiding the perennial question of the carriage.

"Surely it's too far for you? If we had a carriage, I could send it to fetch you."

With a sense of relief, Alinor heard a heavy footstep on the stair. "That you, Ned?"

Ned's first thought on coming in was that Julia Reekie must be quarreling with her mother-in-law, her face was so sulky. She did not rise to greet him but leaned back on the arm of the sofa as if exhausted. Then he saw the pallor of her powdered skin and the rich sheen of her silk dress and realized that she was copying the languor of the ladies of the court, and his nephew, Rob, had escaped a false marriage with the adventuress Livia Avery, who never stopped scheming, for the safety of a woman who did nothing.

He took her gloved fingertips. "Honored."

"Do sit down, Ned," Alinor urged.

He took a chair opposite her at the worktable. "Did Rob come with you, Mrs. Reekie?"

"He went to the warehouse to see his sister, Mrs. Shore," she said. "I can't bear the noise."

Ned took care not to exchange a glance with Alinor. "Can't you?"

"Will you take a hot chocolate, Ned?" Alinor asked.

He rose from his seat. "Nay, I'll have a small ale with Rob in the countinghouse. But I'll send up my lad with your cups."

Julia gave a little cry of alarm and sat up. "Not the native!" she exclaimed. "I beg that he doesn't come in here —"

"Send Susie," Alinor interrupted with a warning look at Ned. "Julia, dear, don't be —"

"What's supposed to be wrong with my lad?" Ned asked quietly.

"I would be so afraid," Julia said. "The things we've heard of them. The way they have gone wild!" She turned to Alinor. "Do you keep him in the house at night? Aren't you afraid he might . . . ? I mean, they can

58

never be trusted."

"Ned!" Alinor cut across his angry retort. To Julia, she said gently: "My dear, you shouldn't believe all that you read in the newssheets. Rowan is our guest, and we are glad to have her."

"Her?" Julia repeated on a rising note. "Never tell me it's a girl?" She shot a horrified glance at Ned. "You brought a native woman into your home?"

Ned folded his arms and watched his sister try to recover.

"Him," Alinor corrected herself. "Well, anyway. You know what I mean! Anyway — Ned, send Susie up with the drinks."

Ned, Alys, and Rob, drinking a cup of small ale in the countinghouse, heard the front door open. "That'll be Johnnie," Alys said. "He comes to do the books every week."

In the narrow hall, Johnnie took off his thick jacket and hat and handed them to Rowan. "Here you are again," he said. "Are you finding your way around London? Do you know the name of this street?"

She nodded. "It's Shad Thames Street."

"Very good," he said. "And I remember due east." He pointed. "Have you been out to see other streets? Have you been over the river to the City?"

"I've been to the market with Tabs."

"The market? What did you think of it? Very busy?"

"It smells of dead food," she said bluntly and made him laugh.

"You should see London Bridge, you should see the Tower of London." He paused. "Shall I —" He broke off. "I could —"

Alys called from the warehouse. "Is that you, Son?"

"I have to go," he said.

Rowan stepped to one side. Still, Johnnie did not go down the hall.

"Do you get a day off?"

"Off?" she repeated. "Off what?"

He realized she did not understand what he meant, and the gulf between their worlds was unbridgeable. "Nothing," he said, and he smiled and left her in the hall.

"Ah, our Company man! Are you rushed off your feet with business?" Rob joked, as Johnnie kissed his mother and shook hands with his great-uncle Ned.

"I'm waiting on a shipment of tea," Johnnie said equably. "I've got nothing to do till it arrives. But I'll take no aspersions from a doctor, whose patients only labor every nine months."

"Did you visit the Gregsons?" Alys asked him.

Johnnie exchanged a glance with Rob. His mother's hopes that he would marry a young woman with a profitable business were well

60

known to everyone. "Not yet. I am to go to dinner next week. But more important than that — I have a letter for you, Ma. From my sister."

Alys exclaimed with pleasure, broke the seal, and read aloud:

Dear Ma and dearest Grandmother,

I am sorry not to have written for so long, we've been busier than usual as a church nearby is changing their hangings and we are chosen to sell their old silks when they buy new, so now I have a warehouse full of dusty old silk altar cloths and beautiful vestments, hangings, curtains for statues, and drapes for tombs that will indeed be worth a fortune when they are cleaned and darned. Felipe is selling, in their place, most of the consignment of silks that Johnnie had shipped to us from his Dutch trader in Japan. I suppose the new king and queen need vestments and altar cloths for the new royal chapels? We hear that they are turning the whole country papist!

Alys broke off. "The rest is about the silks . . . Oh!" she said in quite a different tone. "She says:

I also will send a rather precious consignment — to wit — two beautiful granddaughters for you! If you agree, I should

61

like Mia and Gabrielle to come to you for a long visit. It is very hard for me to give them the girlhood I would like them to have in this city. Girls of good family are kept very strictly at home, and there is no society for young people at all. It is hard for me to find tutors and quite impossible to find anyone to teach science and philosophy to girls. There is almost no education for girls outside the convents. They are both very scholarly girls, which is not easy in Venice, where women are mostly encouraged to religious studies. Gabrielle in particular shows a great interest in herbs and plants — just like my dearest grandmother. Felipe says if they are Venetian girls, then they should be betrothed in two years, married in three, and that would solve the problem with a cradleful of babies by the time they are eighteen — but I say they are English girls and I don't want them married young and their life in the keeping of a husband.

We have talked of this with the girls, and they are eager to come. I always thought that this visit would happen — I did not think it would be so soon!

I will, of course, pay for their keep with you and pay their fees for what tutors you can find for them. Please deduct it from our trade balance with you. They are truly dear girls and no trouble, their only flaw is this terrible cleverness. I think they must have it from you, Ma, with your head for business, and from you, dearest Grandmother, and your love of herbs. For sure, I have never been interested in anything but hats and making money so there should be no blame attached to me for raising girls who want to study things and think about them.

Felipe tells me to warn you what you do, for if you are successful in ridding us of our two girls, we have two boys coming along behind them whom he will send to you as well. David should join the navy for sure, and Luca is very talented in music, at least I think so. But Felipe is just teasing me, for he knows I cannot bear to be parted with any of them. It's such a relief to know that Captain Shore sails regularly between us, it feels as if I am never far from you. And if anything were to go wrong — for a moment — you must send them home to me, whatever it is.

And Ma — do say no if it is too much for you? Please ask Johnnie what he thinks and ask him to send me a note with his opinion. Tell him one of the silks he sent is very lovely. I can sell it very well here, or to let me know if he wants it sent on with Capt. Shore? Yellow with gold thread, and an ell wide and ten long.

I write in haste as a Dutch ship will sail this morning for London and I can send this to you if I get it to the Capt. now — I send you all my love as always, dearest Ma and dearest Grandmama, hoping you are well and the family too, as we are . . . Sarah

"What a riot her brain is," Johnnie said. "And how can you even read it? The last paragraph is scrawled sideways through the rest."

"I like hearing the scramble of her thoughts," his mother said, smiling. "Wouldn't it be wonderful to have her girls to stay here?"

"Julia would be glad to have them in Hatton Garden," Rob put in.

Both Alys and Johnnie ignored the polite lie.

"Can you manage two girls here, Ma?"

"Oh yes, now that we have the second warehouse. Tabs and Susie can sleep over that side and the girls could go in the eaves."

"They'll be used to something a bit grander than servants' rooms," Rob pointed out.

"I won't be in your way for long," Ned offered.

"I think the rooms are the least of your worries. What does she say?" Johnnie consulted the letter. "Philosophy and science? And one of them interested in herbs and plants?"

"What about St. Saviour's?" Rob suggested. "The school is for boys only, of course, but the new master's wife has set up a class for girls in their parlor. They say that she's teaching the same subjects as the boys are learning! And the girls can take lessons with Hester's governess until they start."

"What a good idea!" Alys said, her eyes shining. "They can come on Captain Shore's return voyage. He sails in mid-June. And if you leave Rowan with us, Uncle Ned, she can serve as their maid. She can come out of her boys' clothes and look after the two of them."

"Would she want to do that?" Rob asked doubtfully. "Is she at all trained?"

"She'll do as she pleases," Ned replied stiffly. "She's not to be trained like a dog."

"No, of course . . . I meant no disrespect. Just whether it would suit her? Will you ask her?"

"Alys can ask her, if she wants to," Ned said unhelpfully.

"I'll ask," Johnnie interrupted. "She might feel obliged if it came from Ma."

Alys gathered up the scrawled pages of the letter. "I'll go and read this to Ma and Julia."

"Come and have a look at this barrel of herbs of mine," Ned invited Rob. "I've got a sort of moss that might interest you. The native peoples use it for wounds, it stops bleeding." Ned led Rob through the door into the warehouse as Johnnie crossed the hall and stepped over the stone sill into the kitchen.

Rowan was at the table, an apron around her breeches, her boys' shirtsleeves rolled up, floured to the elbows, inexpertly kneading dough. Tabs was seated at the head of the table.

"Gently! Gently!" she insisted. "You're kneading it, not beating it to death!" She rose to her feet when Johnnie came in. "Master Johnnie," she said with pleasure. "Good to see you. Will you take a glass of small ale? And an apple puff when it comes out the oven? If it isn't crushed flat?"

He smiled at her. "Hello, Tabs. I've just come for a word with young Rowan here."

"Brush the flour off your hands and take off your apron and go with the master into the parlor," Tabs told her.

Rowan followed Johnnie into the front room. It was cool, as the room faced north over the river, the greenish lights dancing on the ceiling as the early summer light reflected off the high tide. Rowan pulled down her shirtsleeves. He thought how unlike an Englishwoman she was: the way she stood in alert silence.

"Mrs. Shore is going to invite her granddaughters from Venice," he told her. At the narrowing of her eyes, he guessed that she did not know of this side of the family and had never even heard of Venice. "Mrs. Shore — my mother, Alys — has a daughter: my sister, Sarah — very dear to me. She lives with her husband and children in Venice, far away from here — more than thirty days' sailing. They have four children and the two oldest, two girls, are coming on a visit.

"If you wish, you could be their maid. If you wish. You're not obliged. But it would give you a trade, and a safe place." He was surprised at himself, taking any trouble over her.

"What would I do?"

"You would take them their breakfasts in the morning and help them wash and dress. You would clean their rooms and wash their linen. You would walk out with them when they wanted to go out, you would carry things for them and run errands. You would help them change their clothes in the evening and put them to bed at night. I suppose you would mend their clothes and arrange their hair."

"They are babies? Little girls, who need help to dress and eat?"

"No, they are young ladies," he said. "They are . . ." He thought for a moment. "Thirteen and twelve years old."

She looked at him with the straight gaze of a young man, as if breeches made her honest in a way that a young lady in a sea of silk and lace and petticoats could never be. "No, I won't do that."

"You would be paid," he told her, more hesitantly. "If you do well, you could go into service, and work your way up."

"Up where?"

He laughed, but then realized it was a genuine question. "Up to another position. With a young lady of higher rank. And then up again. While you worked hard and pleased people you would rise."

"No," she said simply.

"But what else can you do?" he asked her.

"I am one of the People," she told him again. "We are not born to be servants; nor slaves."

"They're not the same thing at all —" he began.

"Would you serve a young lady?" she demanded.

He laughed awkwardly. "Well, really, I could not."

"A young gentleman? Fetch and carry for him, get him dressed, put him to bed? Spend your life in making him comfortable, as if he did not have hands and feet to fetch and carry for himself?"

"No!" he said. "I would not. But I am —" He broke off.

"You're an Englishman," she named him. "You have pride in your milk skin. You have pride in your wealth. You have pride in the things that you know, and no interest in the things that you don't. You would serve nobody, because in your heart you think that nobody is above you."

He could not disagree.

"I'm not saying you're wrong," she said

gently. "But you must know that I am proud — just like you. I am proud of my brown skin and my hair as black and straight as an icicle. I too think that nobody is above me. You are an Englishman — and that seems a very great thing to you; but I am a child of the Dawn-lands. To me, that is better."

"The English are the greatest nation in the world . . ." he started. He could not explain to her the thousands of ships at sea, shipping cargo all around the world, guns to Africa, slaves to the New World, cotton and sugar on the homeward leg, goods to the Americas. His own hugely profitable trades in India: cotton, tea, silk. "You know nothing about my people."

"You know nothing about mine."

"But what will you do?" he demanded, as anxious as if he was the one alone in a strange country. "This is a hard city for young women. My uncle says you can't go back to your home, that your tribe are all dead. How will you live if you don't make money?"

She flinched as he called them a tribe, a dead tribe. "It's not a hard city for me. Nowhere is hard for me but winter."

"What if someone attacks you?"

She hid a smile. "No man puts a hand on me."

"Oho? You can fight?" He meant to tease her; but the grave look she gave him told him that she could fight to the death.

"It is true, there is no home for me to go back to," she conceded. "I shall have to find a way to live in this old world, this world of sunsets." She paused for a moment, as if she realized what she had said. "Ah . . . it is an old world of sunsets."

"All this about the dawn means nothing!" he exclaimed.

"It means nothing to you."

St. James's Palace, London, Spring 1685
The king was closeted with the queen in her privy chamber overlooking the gardens, only Father Mansuet, his confessor, and two ladies-in-waiting in attendance. Livia, striking in a gown of dark blue silk cut low across her creamy shoulders, stood behind the queen, her dark eyes on the king's excited face.

"I shall be master," he gabbled, his face flushed, his wig pushed slightly askew. "I shall be master in my household and father to the nation. Parliament have given me all I need to dominate this rebellious kingdom."

"Have they agreed that men of our faith shall be army officers and MPs and justices of the peace?" Father Mansuet prompted, his eyes on his own hands, clasped as if in prayer, before him. "Men of our faith must take power, so we can bring England to God without opposition."

"Not yet! Not yet! I can't get our people

into the law or into parliament yet. But I have won my own army officered by true believers. Right now, I've got only ten thousand men scattered all around the country, in no state to fight." He laughed excitedly. "But I shall raise an army of true believers and march on Scotland and the Presbyterians myself."

"No!" The queen spoke for the first time, raising herself from her chair. "You can't go."

"Who should lead my army of true believers, but me?"

She compressed her lips on the answer. Everyone knew that the king could not risk his life when he had no heir but girls: first his daughter Mary — ruled by her husband, William of Orange: a dyed-in-the-wool Protestant — and then the Protestant Anne. No Catholic would see the sacred Mass ever again if they took the throne. "What about me?" she demanded. "I was called by God . . . by God . . ." She lost her voice. Livia put an arm around her waist, and James looked at the two beautiful dark-haired women entwined like lovers.

"You shall fulfill His will," he promised.

"Her Majesty will bear a son," Father Mansuet predicted. "A Roman Catholic Prince of Wales."

"But how many ships have landed?" Livia asked. "Argyll's ships?"

The angry glance from the king told her

that he had no idea how many ships had invaded, nor how many men they carried, nor how many men had rushed to join the rebellion when they landed.

"And is James, Duke of Monmouth, with Argyll?" the queen demanded.

"I don't know. I know they've got turncoats and traitors. I ordered that William dismiss Englishmen from his army. I don't want Englishmen marching against France."

"But if they had done nothing wrong . . . ?" she queried.

"Anyway, William did as I ordered. He dismissed them — and now they've gone straight to Monmouth!"

"You ordered that Englishmen should be dismissed from the Dutch army — and they've all gone to Monmouth?" she repeated, disbelievingly.

"I had to! I couldn't have English soldiers fighting the French!" James shouted, covering his mistake with bluster. "King Louis is our only friend in this damned Protestant world! He's the only one I can count on. He is of the true faith, he has promised me funds to restore the faith to England. We are as one: he and I! We are brother monarchs! We are brother Catholics!"

"But everyone in England hates him!" the queen exclaimed. "And to please him, you've given Monmouth an army of experienced English soldiers."

"I didn't know they would go to him! I thought they would just come home."

"They may indeed come home!" she said furiously. "With Monmouth at their head!"

"I'll be ready for them," the king swore. "I'll raise the militia in Scotland, I'll go to the privy council and order them out, right now. I'll call on the north to arm." He turned to Livia. "How many men can your husband muster for my cause in Yorkshire?"

"Hundreds," Livia said firmly.

"I'll come with you to the council." Father Mansuet went to follow him.

"Wait!" Livia said to the priest. "Won't it look as if you are advising the king?"

"Of course I advise him," he said proudly. "We care nothing that they see it!"

The queen watched them leave and waved the ladies-in-waiting away. She turned to Livia. "Only now is he calling out the militia? Though he has known Argyll was sailing for weeks?"

Livia had no answer.

"And anyway — who will the militia fight for: the king or the duke? Where is the loyalty in Yorkshire?"

"Probably for the Protestant duke," Livia reluctantly spoke the truth. "All of the Yorkshire spinners and weavers are Protestant, many of them fought before for Cromwell. They've faced a royal army before. They have no fear of it, they have no respect. They're independent men, their own masters, they all follow their own consciences, they obey no one."

"So, when you told the king that your husband could raise hundreds . . . ?"

"I didn't know what to say . . ."

"Everyone does that!" the queen exclaimed. "No one tells him anything that he will not like! Just like his father, King Charles. He thought he was safe, they put him on trial, and he expected to speak — in the very hall where we went to open parliament! I probably stood in his footprints! I probably stood in his bloodstained footprints! He did not know, until it was too late, that people hated him!"

Her terror was infectious. "It will never happen again!" Livia promised.

"You heard the king. He doesn't know. They've hated me since I came here, they burned an effigy the day I arrived! My wedding was held in secret for fear of the mob. They hate Catholic queens. They fired on Queen Henrietta! They would have killed her. She had to flee for her life!"

"She ran away?"

"She had to! I will have to! If Argyll and Monmouth are on the march, then I'll have to go to France like she did. Her husband could not protect her and neither can mine!"

Reekie Wharf, London, Spring 1685

Johnnie, surprised at himself, was drawn back to the warehouse within the week, and found his uncle Ned on the quayside with a cargo manifest in his hand.

"Has my ma set you to work?" Johnnie asked, crossing the cobbles.

"No one's idle in this house. But actually, I am doing nothing more than holding this while your ma goes to find a missing barrel. I am the equivalent of a book stand."

"It was you I wanted to see," Johnnie said awkwardly.

"Here I am," Ned said, and when the younger man hesitated, he said: "Still here."

"Yes, I know. It's . . . it's about your lad . . . about Rowan, I mean. Your er . . ."

"About Rowan," Ned prompted.

"I keep thinking about her!" Johnnie exclaimed, and then flushed. "Not like that! I mean, I have been thinking about her position. Here. And I've found her a place if she wants it."

"That's good of you," Ned said carefully, looking at the younger man. "Good of you to take the trouble."

"It's no trouble. I've found her a place at a school, a dame school. She'd be a pupil in lessons and earn her keep by helping with

76

the housework. I thought she should learn to read and write there. If she showed aptitude, she could perhaps become a pupil teacher. She obviously doesn't want to be a servant."

"Why are you so interested in Rowan?" Ned asked.

The younger man flushed. "It's not anything . . ." He trailed off. "I just think she should have a chance," he said. "Coming as she does from . . . over there. And everything must be so strange for her here. She's got such courage . . . Anyway, what do you plan for her? And what happens when you leave?"

"I don't have any plans," Ned admitted. "I bought her out of slavery on the dockside with no plan but to save her life. I thought she'd find her own way. Perhaps she'd take to your idea. You'd have to ask her."

"You'd let her go?"

"I don't own her. She'll do as she pleases."

"But she needs a protector," Johnnie suggested.

"I doubt that. Anyway — tell her about the place." Ned hesitated. "Be warned: she may not be grateful — her people don't tally up favors like we do."

"But I can speak to her?" the younger man confirmed.

Ned waved towards the warehouse. "She's in the yard."

Johnnie nodded and went down the alley at the side of the house to enter the yard through the open gates.

Rowan was squatting on her haunches, carefully picking the yellow buds off a bed of herbs and putting them in a basket. The sweet scent was all around her, her fingernails stained green. She heard footsteps on the cobbles and rose up in one supple movement to confront the intruder. He saw her relax as she recognized him.

"I've come to see you," he said.

She did not curtsey as a young woman should, nor did she bow as a servant should. She just stood waiting to hear why he had come. Now he was before her, he did not know what to say. Her dark gaze was fixed on his face and — unlike an English girl — she did not smile or help him speak. She waited as if the silence was not awkward.

"I've found a place that might suit you," he said. "You'd be attached to a school for young girls. You would have to do some cleaning and perhaps . . ." He looked down at her basket of flower heads. "Perhaps garden work? But you would be taught to read and write and you might learn a trade."

"In London?" she asked.

"Yes. In this parish. St. Olave's Church has a school for boys, and girls are taught by the clergyman's wife. They need a pupil teacher who would help with lessons and with running the vicarage."

"Why?" she inquired.

"It would give you a way to earn a living. It would protect you from strangers and . . . You would be chaperoned by a good woman and live in her house. You would dress in proper clothes and attend church."

"No," she corrected him. "Why have you found this place for me?"

"I'd like to help you." He could hardly believe that she was so composed while he was stumbling over his words and shifting from foot to foot, as if the favor would be her gift to him. She was in his mother's yard and in his great-uncle's service, but she seemed blind to her dependency. Johnnie, a businessman and the son of a wharfinger, realized she could not be bought or sold; and he had thought everything had a price.

"Do you want me as your woman?" she asked bluntly.

He blushed at her bawdiness. "No! Don't say that!" he said hastily. "You can't speak like that. In our world, you can't say something like that."

She looked puzzled. "Then how does a woman tell her man she wants him?"

He shook his head, loosened his collar against a sudden heat. "She doesn't. She doesn't speak of such things. A young lady waits for her father . . . to tell her . . . that a marriage is arranged. She cannot speak for herself."

Rowan shook her head, quite baffled. "We

just say. A woman makes her choice and tells him."

"You're not in your country now!" Johnnie snatched off his hat and ran his hand through his hair. "You're under the protection of my great-uncle. He will answer for you."

"I am not his woman," she pointed out.

Johnnie cast an anxious look at the open kitchen door for fear that Tabs or Susie was listening. "No! I know that!"

"Oh — you don't want me?" she asked as if she were merely trying to get something clear.

"I do — I would — but I must not —" He was choking on his words. "I may not say . . . I have no intentions towards . . . this was an offer of charity . . . not a proposition. I would not insult you or my uncle by suggesting . . . I would never . . . in my mother's house!"

They stood in silence; he was burning with embarrassment and she was perfectly calm.

She shrugged her shoulders, as if she gave up the puzzle. "I don't understand you people," she said flatly. "But I am not free."

"You're betrothed to someone?" He swallowed his dismay. "You're married?"

"Ned Ferryman saved my life. Until I repay the debt to him, I owe him my life. I am not free to leave him nor go to any man. It is a blood debt."

He nearly laughed with relief. "Oh, that doesn't matter. He wouldn't think that . . ."

She was completely serious. "It does not

matter what he thinks, or what you think. He saved my life — until the debt is repaid, I am his."

"He won't have a slave," Johnnie reminded her.

"I am not enslaved, I am indebted."

"If you were not indebted, would you like me?" he asked, struggling to find words. "As a friend? I cannot offer any . . . as a friend?"

"I have not seen enough white men to know one of you from another. And most of you are savages." She picked up her basket and patted the calendula flowers.

"Savages!" He repeated the word, which was used for her people, not his.

"Killers. Rapists. Men with power but without law."

Johnnie realized that she had survived events that he had never even heard of. "I like you, Rowan," he said carefully. "And I will be your friend. I will help you in any way that I can."

She nodded gravely. "When I know what I want, I will tell you," she promised. "Until then, I will go where Ned Ferryman goes, until my debt is paid."

"He might lead you into danger," Johnnie warned. "You don't understand. He is not a good guide for you. He doesn't believe in kings, he doesn't believe in masters —"

He broke off when he saw her mischievous smile. "But neither do I. My Massasoit —

81

my king — is dead. I will never serve a master, I shall go with your uncle Ned until I am free and I know what I want to do."

"And what then?" he demanded. "What — when you know what you want to do?" He was dazzled by her easy confidence:

"Then I will do that."

Amsterdam, Holland, Spring 1685

It was not hard for Ned, with Rowan like a silent shadow at his heels, to track down James, Duke of Monmouth, to his inn on the Martelaarsgracht of Amsterdam.

"What kind of land is this with no rivers but all the water between banks of stone?" Rowan demanded, horrified. "Is it like Johnnie said — all street and no sky?"

"They're great ones for building, the Hollanders," Ned said. "All of this here will once have been tidelands, waterland. But they build a wall against the sea, and then pump the land behind it dry. Every street is a quayside in this town." It was impossible to explain to one of the People, who lived on an unending continent, that there was not enough land to be had.

"They live all the time in these . . . ?" She had no word for the row of low-browed houses that scowled over the narrow stinking canal.

"Aye," Ned said.

"They have no woods? They have no fields?

82

They are so very poor, they don't even have forests?"

"No! This is the wealthiest trading country in the world. They used to own all the wealth of the East until we set up our own East India Company — the one my nephew, Johnnie, works for. Even now, they still hold more than half of the trade."

"They choose this?" she asked incredulously, gesturing to the narrow door that fronted the canal and the glazed window beside it that gave them a glimpse of a low-ceilinged wood-paneled room, and a closed stove with a blue-and-white-tiled surround, a table before the window dressed with a Turkey rug. Ned thought it a fine stone-built house. He stepped back to admire the gables and the upper windows and the painted sign of the merchant householder.

"To an Amsterdammer, that's a grand house," Ned told her. "Now, hold your tongue, we're going into an alehouse to meet a lord and his council."

He gestured her to follow him down the half dozen stone steps to a narrow wooden door into the wood-floored, wood-paneled public room of the Karpershoek Inn. She hesitated at the head of the stairs, peering into the darkness.

"It's below the water?"

"Follow me," Ned said over his shoulder.

A man was sitting at the great table at the

back of the room, half a dozen men around him. A beam of sunlight, crossing the gloomy room from the high windows, illuminated the shine on his dark brown ringlets over the white lace collar. Ned recognized, without pleasure, the Stuart family charm and the Stuart good looks. "Wait here," he said to Rowan. "Better that you hear nothing."

Rowan stood still beside the stubby newel post of the stairs. Ned, glancing back, saw that she melted into the gloom of the room, just as she would have disappeared into trees when hunting at her home. Ned doffed his hat and approached the table.

The duke looked up, a slight smile on his face. "Come in," he said, as if he were in his private house.

"I'm Ned Ferryman," Ned said with a little bow. "From New England. Come to enter your service, if your cause is just and you'll have me."

"I've no money to pay you," the duke said honestly.

"I'd serve for the cause alone; if it's a good one."

"It seems good to me, but I won't command any man's conscience."

"You would keep England in the reformed faith?"

"I'm the Protestant prince, everyone knows that." He nodded at the tap boy, who was standing with a cloth over his arm and a jug of beer. "Pour this good man a drink."

The boy set a mug before Ned and went out, closing the door behind him.

"I'll serve you if you wear the green ribbon," Ned said. Green was the color of the Levellers, the radicals of the old Cromwell army. These days it was worn by the men who drank at the King's Head in London, talking of freedom and of the rights of men. To every Englishman, it meant the right to his own religion, to his family, to his own land, and legal limits on the power of the king.

"We're all of that mind. D'you know anyone here that can vouch for you?" The duke gestured around the table. He smiled at a fresh-faced young man of nineteen. "Not William Hewling here. But anyone else?"

"I've been away from England for many years. Half my comrades are dead of old age! Anyone who was in my company at Naseby might remember me." Ned hesitated. "I don't know that's a recommendation to you, sir: I was fighting your grandfather Charles I." Ned glimpsed the Stuart mournful smile.

"A civil war is always a family matter. I'll be taking up arms against my uncle, an ordained king. I shall be the first Stuart to deny the power of the king. I shall be a Leveller Stuart."

"My father was a major in the New Model Army." A man of about twenty years spoke up from the foot of the table. "Major Wade?

D'you know him? A one-armed man, but he could ride a horse as well as any other."

Ned grinned at the trap that had been laid for him. "The Major Wade I knew had two arms," he said. "A godly man, name of John. Family were great men in Bristol. Cursed like a stevedore when he was angry."

"That's him." Nathaniel Wade nodded. He glanced at Monmouth. "Probably is who he says he is," he said grudgingly.

"I've made covenants with these men already," the duke replied. "I've said that if I succeed in England and the throne is offered me, I'll take it, only if the people of England want a king. If they want a Lord Protector, I'll offer to serve. But it shall be for the people to decide."

"You'll hold parliaments every year?" Ned persisted. "And not when it suits you?"

The duke nodded and waited for more.

"And give every landholder a vote?"

"If the parliament requests it."

"And impose no religion or belief on any man or woman, but let each consult his own conscience? No imprisonment without just cause. No picking of judges to suit yourself. No new taxation?"

The duke nodded again.

"Then I offer you my service," Ned said. "Such as it is."

"I accept your service," the duke said. He gestured for Ned to sit at the table. "Did you

86

train men for the New England militia?"

"Aye," Ned said. "And in England, in the first civil war. I can drill foot soldiers and teach the use of a musket."

"D'you have any funds?" a handsome man demanded from the end of the table. "For all this talk of kings — and some of us would have no kings ever again — we need a royal fortune to kit out a ship." He hesitated. "I'm Thomas Dare, from Devon."

"I've no more than I stand up in, and a few coins in my pocket. I can pay my way and buy my weapons."

"D'you have family? Tenants? Servants?"

"I'm a single man."

"You've got a slave," another man observed in a rolling west-country drawl, glancing at Rowan, who stood still and silent by the stairs at the door. "Can you sell him?"

"He's free," Ned said. "He travels with me until he wishes to leave."

"We're desperate short of funds," Thomas Dare explained. "I'm Paymaster — but I've nothing to save or spend. And we have to hire ships and buy arms, and pay for munitions, banners and favors, and we're taking a printing press to print the muster . . ."

The duke gave a little grimace and plunged his hand into the deep pocket of his richly embroidered jacket. He brought out a fat purse and slid it across the table.

"My honor is in this purse," he said. "Make

sure you get full value for it."

Thomas Dare, who had been a goldsmith in his home of Taunton, untied the purse and peeped inside. He let out a quiet whistle and tied the purse again and put it in his own pocket. "Her ladyship's jewels?" he asked the duke.

Monmouth nodded. "She has given up everything for me," he said quietly. "And now the very rings from her fingers, and from her own mother's neck."

"I should get enough from this and from the sale of your goods to pay the rest of the fee for the ships and buy arms," Dare said, rising to his feet.

"Take Mr. Ferryman with you," Monmouth said. "He can check the guns. And I'll write to my friends again, someone must lend us more money. I'll pawn the rest of my goods." He frowned. "I'll clear the house, even the linen from the beds."

"And quickly! We're promised to sail within days," another man reminded him. "Argyll is counting on support; we can't fail him."

"I'll pawn the jewels," Dare promised, nodding to Ned to follow him. "And we'll buy the arms. I'll meet you at the quayside at Texel tomorrow afternoon, sire."

Reekie Wharf, London, Spring 1685
Matthew was eating his breakfast at the scrubbed table in the kitchen warehouse. Alys

poured him a mug of small ale and took her seat opposite him. For a moment she admired his profile, as straight and beautiful as any of the Greek statues they sold, a handsome youth on the edge of manhood. "D'you get enough to eat? Do they give you a good dinner at the Inns of Court?" she asked.

"You can see, I'm not fading away," Matthew replied.

She smiled; he was fifteen years old but already the top of his head was level with her own neat white cap.

"You're all legs," she said fondly. "There's nowt on you. Will you come home on Friday evening?"

"Course," he said, his mouth filled with bread and beef.

She hesitated. "Have you heard from your mother?"

He took a long draft of small ale. "Not since she wrote to me that she was coming to the queen's court, weeks ago. Have you?"

"I don't expect to hear from her," Alys said flatly. "If she invites you to visit, will you go?"

"I'm curious. I've not seen her since she visited us when I was ten and she was come and gone in an hour. I can only remember her carriage, and the cake she gave me. I wouldn't know her if I passed her in the street."

"Oh, you'd know her soon enough," Alys said wryly.

He looked up at the woman who had been his foster mother since infancy. "She's so beautiful?"

"Not even that. She has . . ."

"Style? Italian style?"

"She takes your attention," Alys said. "If you passed her in the street, she'd take your attention."

"She smiles at you?"

"She's more likely to look down her nose at you for having the nerve to glance at her."

"She's proud?"

"Very."

"Well, she's not likely to condescend to visit me — a little 'puny' at Lincoln's Inn." He smiled at the nickname for the junior scholars. "And even less to come here. So I'll have to wait for an invitation to court, if I hope to see her." He took one last gulp of small ale and rose from the table.

"I'll come with you to the water stairs." Alys folded her lips on a warning that his mother might disappoint him.

He left the dishes as they were and went into the hall. His jacket was on the chair, his hat beside it, and a satchel of papers — his legal studies — on the floor. He shrugged into his jacket and placed his hat at a rakish angle on his long curly hair. Alys put her hands on his shoulders and he bent his head like a boy, for her to kiss his forehead.

"God bless you, Son," she said. "Work hard

and keep out of trouble." She hesitated; the students of the Inns of Court were notoriously rowdy and hard drinking. "You are learning?"

"Ma!" he protested. "We can't all be like Johnnie and live for nothing but work!"

"At least don't be a spendthrift!" she replied.

"D'you think I have folly in my veins?"

She feared worse; but she shook her head. "I know you're going to be a good man. You're our boy before you are anyone else's."

He tapped his hat more firmly on his head and took up his satchel. "I'll be home late Friday. Don't wait up for me."

"You be home late, and you'll find the door bolted against you," she threatened, smiling. "I'll have no wild young men hammering on the door at midnight."

He laughed, knowing she would never lock him out. "Come on, then. I can't be late now. I am to listen to a pleading in the law from one of the senior scholars, and at a crucial moment I have an important task: I am to hand him a pen."

"That's your only work for the day?"

"That's my greatest moment," he corrected her. "All eyes will be on me."

They walked arm in arm upriver along the quay past their own ship, to where the Horsleydown Stairs ran from the quay to the lapping water below.

"But you are learning?" Alys confirmed.

"I am, but everyone says, it's not what it was. Some scholars do nothing but dine there, never open a book. Some of the qualified men don't even use their chambers but let them out to visitors to London like an inn. But some of us read in the library, and I am learning. I eat my dinners and I listen to the discourse, I'll serve my terms and maybe catch someone's eye and get a pupilage. I will come out of this a lawyer, Ma. I'll be able to defend you, whatever you do."

"I'm a hardened criminal," Alys confessed. "We need a lawyer in the family." She hugged him good-bye at the top of the stairs and stood on the quay as he went down the wet steps to signal to a passing wherry. The boatman pulled alongside and Matthew climbed aboard, settled himself in the stern, and raised his hand to her. She watched him go, the wherryman pulling against the ebbing tide, upstream to the wealth of the City where Johnnie worked, to the Inns of Court where Matthew studied, and beyond them, to the palace where his mother had lived for weeks and never sent for him.

Alys turned and went back to the warehouse. Her husband's ship, *Sweet Hope,* was at the quayside, and she could see him on board, checking the loading. She waved to him, as she stepped over the stone sill which kept high-tide floodwater from the front door, and climbed the steep wooden stairs to her mother's bedroom, which overlooked the quay at the front and the River Neckinger at the side. Alinor was seated at the round table, windows wide open, herbs and muslin purses spread around the table.

"Has he gone?" she asked, glancing up from her work as Alys came into the room.

Alys sniffed at the fresh smell of dried mint and another perfume, more exotic.

"Sassafras, mint, and scurvy grass," Alinor told her. "Slavers' tea."

Alys took a handful of the mixture and buried her nose in it. "Delicious," she said. She put down the herbs and sat opposite her mother, took up a purse, and tipped in a measure of the dried leaves as Alinor went on working, her thin hands deft from long practice. "He told me he'd be late Friday night as he's dining with friends."

"Cut his allowance," Alinor joked with a warm smile at her daughter. "If he can treat his friends, you're giving him too much."

"I don't want him to look poor beside them. If he's to go among gentlemen scholars, I don't want him behindhand."

"Don't you spoil him," Alinor advised. "You and Rob didn't turn out badly, and neither of you ever had more than a ha'penny in your pocket."

Alys flushed. "We turned out all right in the end," she emphasized. "There's no comparison, Ma — not between the tidelands and the wharf: now that we've got the ship and my Abel in partnership with us — Johnnie trading in the East India Company and Sarah sending us such goods from Venice!"

"I'm grateful for our blessings."

"Don't forget what it was really like," Alys reminded her. "We never ate meat unless I'd poached it from the Peachey lands. We ate fish when you caught it. We ate butter and cheese when you were given it instead of wages. White bread was a rare treat at harvesttime, cream was something you skimmed for others. It wasn't that you chose not to spoil us — you could barely feed us! I've sworn that I'll never be poor again, and we never will." She rapped on the wooden table for luck. "It's worse than ill-health," she said. "It ruins everything."

"It's just —" Alinor broke off. "The sky over the harbor," she said, her voice full of longing. "The seeping of the water over the shore at high tide. My own parents buried in the churchyard, their names over their resting place. The stile into the churchyard where the roses grow. The oak tree that bends over the mire and the green of the water under the green leaves."

"It'd be all changed," Alys pointed out. "The Peachey family have all died out and the manor gone to the crown. We don't even know who's got our ferry now. We'll have been forgotten."

Alinor smiled. "Someone will have made up stories about us," she said. "As if we were never real at all. As if we just washed in and away again with the tide."

"What d'you think they say?" Alys asked smiling.

"Oh — a woman who danced with fairies and ran away with a merman? A wise woman who paid her debt in faerie gold? A woman swam as a witch and could not drown?"

Alys shivered as if she was cold though the sunshine still shone through the window into the little room. "Let's not think of it. When's Uncle Ned coming back?" she turned the talk. "Has he really gone to join Argyll in Scotland?"

"Monmouth," Alinor said shortly. "He's gone to the duke."

Alys looked down at her husband's ship below. Lumpers were tossing hessian sacks of woolen cloth, one to another, across the quay for stowing in the deep hold. Alys could calculate to the nearest shilling the value of the boat, the value of the load, the likely profit from a good sale in Venice, the value of the artworks and luxury goods that her daughter, Sarah, would send on the return voyage. Her constant calculation of value was not driven by greed but the dread of ruin. "If Uncle Ned is taken for treason we would lose everything," she said very quietly.

"He won't name us," Alinor said gently. "He's promised."

"He'd have done better to promise to have nothing to do with it at all!" Alys exclaimed.

"Aye. So you say. But all his life Ned has been a parliament man. Before you were even born, Alys. He's always been for the Church of England and the people of England. He's bound to fight against a king who's lived in foreign parts for most of his life, is a declared papist, and has a foreign papist wife."

"Still crowned King of England," Alys said stubbornly.

"So was his father," Alinor said cheerfully. "And your uncle Ned saw him beheaded and came home and told us all about it: and we were glad."

"Hush," Alys said, turning from the window. "I won't have a word of it in this house. It's nothing to us! Trade is good, the country is quiet, they're still rebuilding after the fire, and everyone wants our stonework and statues for their houses and gardens, our art for their galleries, and our silk for their walls. Even your tea sells faster than you can make it for the slaving ships. We've got nothing against this king. He can pray as he likes, and as long as he doesn't tax like a papist, I won't hear a word against him."

"You won't hear a word against him from me," Alinor pointed out mildly. "I'm not the ranting sort."

Alys was forced to laugh at her mother, sitting so quietly behind her table with her pile of sweet-smelling herbs and her muslin purses. "You!" she said. "You've got a wild streak in you, Ma — and I see it in my uncle Ned, and in our Sarah when it took her to Venice, and I pray to God that I never see it in Johnnie or Matthew."

Alinor did not deny the wildness. "It was a long time ago — men questioning their king, women questioning their husbands, and everyone questioning their God. Everyone thought that anything could happen. Everyone was drunk with questions."

"Those times are gone," Alys told her severely. "We all want peace now and a sober life."

"Not all of us," Alinor warned her with a gleam of a smile. "Some of us would be glad to be drunk with questions all over again."

Amsterdam, Holland, Spring 1685
Ned and Thomas Dare, followed by Rowan, turned into a dark doorway and went down a short flight of stairs into a metalwork shop. The forge was blazing bright in the yard outside, and the workshop was ringing like a belfry with the noise of men hammering hot iron. The acrid smell of charcoal smoke drifted into the low-ceilinged room.

"Take a good look at the muskets before I pay," Thomas Dare told him. "Put aside anything faulty. We only want the very best."

Ned had seen colonial-made muskets blow off a rifleman's hand. "The lad knows good workmanship," he remarked.

"I thought they weren't allowed weapons?"

"We only sell them faulty ones," Ned said with grim humor. "That's how he knows."

The owner of the shop greeted Thomas, nodded to Ned, and waved them to a pile of muskets ready to be wrapped in sacking and packed into boxes. There were more than a thousand, piled in the corner of the room. Ned made a soundless whistle with his lips and Rowan glanced at him.

"Check one in every ten," he told her.

"You'll find they're good," the forgemaster said as he came over, his leather apron stained with scorch marks and his hands rough with old burns. "I sell my muskets to the Dutch East India Company — they don't pay me to fail!"

"They better be," Thomas Dare replied. "I'll leave you here, Ned, while I get this purse pawned."

"Very well." Ned and Rowan pulled weapons from the stack, checking the sighting, peering down the powder pan, and moving the trigger. They tried the ramrod down the barrels to ensure they were straight. They worked their way through the weapons, and as they passed them to one side, one of the smiths came in and wrapped them in sacking and packed them into wooden crates and nailed them shut.

Ned's head was half deafened by the noise of the yard by the time they had checked the whole pile, and Rowan was pale under the bronze of her skin.

"All good?" Thomas Dare demanded, darkening the room as he came in the doorway.

"All but those." Ned indicated the handful of weapons that had faults.

Thomas Dare handed over a heavy purse; the forgemaster tipped the coins into his scales and weighed them, pulling one or two out to bite in his teeth to see that they had the softness of true gold. Then he and Dare shook hands, and he promised that the weapons should be delivered to the quay at Texel at once.

Dare, Ned, and Rowan emerged with relief into the sunlight of the street.

"What now?" Ned asked.

"Leather jackets," Dare replied. "We need a thousand; they're being made at the tanners' canal, at Jordaan. Shop in the name of Jan Muis — sign outside is a mouse. You can get them, pay for them, and get them delivered to the ship. And powder horns, get as many as you can for the money."

He reached into his pocket, took out a purse, hefted it in his hand, and passed it over to Ned. "See if you can get the price down, for the Lord's sake. Check everything, only pay for good work."

Ned nodded.

"And there's a special leather jacket for his lordship on order. Make sure they deliver them together to the *Helderenberg,* on the dock at the Island of Texel. You'd better go with them. I'll meet you there."

Lincoln's Inn, London, Spring 1685
The usher brought a note to Matthew when he was studying in his room, the window thrown open for air, the sultry stink of the City drifting in.

"Lady sent this," he said shortly.

Matthew lifted his head from his books. "A lady?" He dropped his pen, where it splattered black ink on the case that he was preparing to argue — *Soledad v. Timmings* — and took the note. It was addressed to him as Matteo da Picci, and as soon as he saw the name, in the beautiful script, he knew it was from her.

> Son,
> I would be obliged to you if you would meet me at the coffeehouse at Serle Court.
> I will wait only half an hour.
> Your mother — Nobildonna Livia Avery

Matthew pushed back his chair and

snatched up his jacket, thrusting his arms into the sleeves. A glance in the looking glass over his bed showed a handsome young face, half man, half boy. He crammed his pupil's hat on his long curling hair and crossed the little room in one stride.

"When did you get this?" he threw over his shoulder to the usher who waited on the stair.

"Just five minutes ago, sir," the man said. "A lady, with her maid behind her."

Matthew clattered down the winding stone stair, his hand dropping from one worn wooden peg to another on the central stone pillar, and ducked his head under the narrow stone doorway.

Matthew's rooms were in Gatehouse Court, a tall redbrick building trimmed with pale sandstone that had seemed overwhelmingly grand to him when he first took his room as a student to the inn. Now he did not notice the buildings set in the huge well-kept gardens, as he pulled his jacket straight on his shoulders and strode, long-legged, across the paved courtyard, through the deep arch into Serle Court, where the stonemasons were carving blocks for the new buildings in one corner and builders were tying wooden poles of scaffolding together nearby. Even from the courtyard Matthew could smell the roasting coffee beans and the rich smell of yeast from brewing ale. He pulled off his hat as he ducked his head under the doorway and opened the door on his right.

The place was quiet; Mr. Hart, the owner, looked up but did not stir from his stool for a mere puny. Only a couple of clerks were seated at the big central table, spread with pamphlets and newspapers. A lawyer and his client were in one corner discussing their case in low tones.

"Good day, Mr. Hart," Matthew said politely, looking past him to the interior.

A veiled lady was seated at a table at the back of the room, her maid standing behind her like a guard. Before her stood a tiny cup of strong coffee. Matthew skidded to a halt and watched her put back her veil, lift the cup, take a sip of coffee, and release her veil to hide her face again. He had seen nothing but rouged lips. His heart thudded at the realization that his mother, his beautiful mysterious mother, had finally come for him.

"The lady is here for you?" Mr. Hart rapidly modified his view of Matthew's unimportance.

"Yes." He walked across the wooden floor, conscious of the creak of his shoes, and stood before her table, her letter in his hand. He thought he must look like a child, summoned to stand before his schoolmaster.

"My lady, you sent for me?" His voice sounded unsteady in his own ears. He flushed. "I am Matthew," he said, and now he was too loud, bellowing like a fool.

She swept back her veil and pinned it on her hat with one swift gesture, as if she were ready to reveal herself to him. Matthew stared into a face that he felt that he knew, that he had somehow always known. She was unforgettable. Thick dark hair was piled off her unlined forehead to tumble in curls to her shoulders, dark eyebrows were arched in interrogation, dark eyes raked him up and down. Her red lips curved into a conspiratorial smile, as if the two of them shared some kind of secret. Dimly, he supposed that they did.

He scanned her face for similarities to his own and found them. Her eyebrows slanted up a little at the ends, as his did. Her eyes were as dark as his, the two of them — mother and son — had the same classically beautiful profile, but his smile was wide and frank, his face was open; hers was veiled even when the lace was put aside.

"Ah, so you are my son," she said. He heard the lilt of her Italian accent, carefully preserved after fifteen years in England. "I would have known you anywhere."

He made an awkward bow, and she rose from the table and put her hands lightly on his shoulders and drew him towards her, kissed his forehead like a blessing, and then — like an Italian — kissed him on both cheeks. Her perfume, a light scent of roses, brushed his memory.

She stepped back to inspect him, as if calculating how best she should treat him. She saw the flush in his cheeks and realized that he was still a boy, a youth, sheltered by a loving foster family, kept from the temptations of the City and the dangers of the world. He might be smartly dressed and handsome, he might be studying law; but he was no match for a woman of her sharp acquisitive wits.

"So . . ." She was reassured. She took her chair and gestured that he should sit opposite her. "So, we meet again. Do you remember me at all?"

"Very slightly," he stumbled.

"Of course, it was a long time ago. You may sit down, my dear boy, my dearest son. *Caro figlio.* You speak Italian?"

At his downcast face she laughed. "Of course you do not. How should you learn? But you are educated? I pay the fees, you know? You read Latin at least? And speak French, I suppose?"

He nodded. "I didn't know you paid . . ."

"Well, yes! The good women of the warehouse could never afford it and would not have known what school you should attend, or how a gentleman should be raised. I took care of all of that. You have to have guarantors to enter the Inns — they're called 'manucaptors' — I provided them too."

"They never said . . . I didn't know." He

105

flushed, angry at himself for blindly assuming that his foster mothers had provided for him in a world they had never known.

"I doubt they speak of me at all! Do they? And never of what they owe me!" Her musical laugh made Mr. Hart look up, and at her gesture, he came over with a fresh pot of coffee and a cup for Matthew.

"They don't," Matthew admitted. "But I thought that was your wish? I thought you told them to raise me and never trouble you?"

"Allora!" she exclaimed. "I see you are a lawyer in the making indeed. *Caro,* I was in no case to issue instructions. I was trapped between the wishes of my new husband and the will of the stubborn old lady. They would have nothing to do with each other, and I had to find a safe haven for my beloved only child, while I made my new marriage."

"For fourteen years?" he queried.

She shot a quick look at him as if assessing his tone. "You feel that I should have sent for you earlier? Would you not have been torn between the women of the warehouse and me? Between two worlds and secure in neither? Was it not better to let them give you a childhood — an English childhood — of great safety and peace?"

"Yes . . ." he said uncertainly.

"And so that is what I did. You lived with them under their name — Reekie — only I cannot say it! So I call you Picci, da Picci for

106

my title. And only now that you are a young man, a proper young man, and I am free of the demands of my husband and the manor and Yorkshire, can I visit you and see that my son has grown, and what we might be to each other."

He felt slow and stupid. "What we might be?"

"Yes, of course, I want to help you to make your way in the world, and I am sure that you would want to see me rise."

"I thought you . . ." Under her bright gaze he found his mouth was dry and took a gulp of coffee. It was scalding hot. He swallowed, feeling the burn go down his gullet. He flushed scarlet at the pain and blinked tears from his eyes.

"You thought I had risen?" Livia guessed, ignoring his discomfort. "Toll-loll! You must know I was a great lady in Venice, of the Fiori family, and then I came to England and married Sir James and became a great lady in Yorkshire, and now I am a great lady in London — a friend to the Queen of England! So, yes! I have risen. And I continue to rise —" She broke off and snatched a quick look at him. "But these are troubled times and I need to know that you are with me. As I work for our good."

"You are working for our good?" he queried.

"Always," she assured him. "When my

dearest friend your foster mother and her mother agreed to take you in, I knew you would be safe with them. But I knew too that the day would come when I would come back for you and make you my own again."

She was unstoppable. He felt his head spinning and his throat hurt.

"I won't leave them."

"Of course not! It would be most churlish. They have been as my nurserymaids, they have been as rockers for you. But I am your mother — that was never forgotten. And I will open doors for you that would otherwise be distant dreams. I will take you to court, you shall meet the king and queen." She assessed the impact she was having on him. "You want to be a lawyer?" she asked abruptly.

"Yes . . ." he said. "Or at any rate some post —"

"There you are then!" she said triumphantly. "I shall find you a post. None of them at the wharf could do so! But now tell me — does the wharf have its own ship now? Alys married Captain Shore, did she not? He still has his ship?"

"Yes," he said.

"Very good, very good. And this ship — it is in London now?"

"Yes."

"For how long?"

"I don't know. They're loading."

"And if I wanted to take passage I could go?"

"I suppose so. They often take passengers."

She smiled at him. "You will be puzzled by all this, I know, Matteo. But I need you to trust me."

The Italian version of his name, spoken lovingly in her accent, startled him. He felt that he had heard her say his name in that caressing voice, through his dreams, for all of the fourteen years that he had answered to Matthew.

"You cannot trust me yet," she said understandingly. "But you will. It may be that I need your help in a matter of life and death. You may be able to save me, your own mother, and . . ." She leaned forward and lowered her voice so that he had to lean towards her to hear her whisper, "the Queen of England herself!"

He could feel her breath on his cheek, he could smell the sweet dark scent of coffee.

"The queen needs a ship?"

She sat back and smiled at his stunned face.

"Because of the invasion?"

"Of course, I cannot say! But you speak to Alys and to Captain Shore and tell them we may need two cabins, perhaps at once, perhaps in some weeks' time, and I will send to you if I need you."

"I may tell them why?"

"As much as you think safe. As little as you can."

"Won't the king provide for her safety? What about the navy?"

She shrugged. "Oh, perhaps! But if he is away fighting with his army? And who should provide for me if not my own boy?" She rose from the table and pulled down her veil from her hat, so her face was hidden.

"Your husband?" he suggested weakly. "Shouldn't he . . ."

She laughed. "He doesn't have a ship and — *allora!* — you do!"

Her maid, who had been standing behind her, came forward and offered her arm. Livia turned to Matthew who stood, quite stunned, before her.

"I shall come again in a few days," she promised, as if he had asked for her. "We shall meet here."

He made a little bow. "As you wish, your ladyship," he said.

She gave him her gloved hand to kiss. He put his lips to the warm silk.

"You may call me Lady Mother," she told him. *"Signora Madre."*

Texel Island, Holland, Spring 1685
The *Helderenberg* rocked in the strong onshore wind, with two smaller ships moored nearby, loaded with weapons, armor, and uniforms for officers who were waiting in England, banners for the crowds, a printing press to publish the duke's manifesto, a printer to set the type, barrels of the rusty brown water of the island, famous for good-keeping on long voyages, barrels of wine, small ale, crates of fresh food, and two brace of hens to lay eggs for the duke's breakfast.

Eighty-three men were mustered to sail in the invasion, some dismissed from William of Orange's army to follow the beloved duke, exiles from King James's England, his lordship's own servants who would die for him, and only one other nobleman: Lord Grey of Werke, who had been set on overturning the monarchy for all his life.

"But never heard a shot fired in anger," Ned said quietly to Samuel Venner, a veteran who had served under Monmouth against the French in the Dutch War.

"He's gentry," Venner replied. "So he can ride a horse, can't he? Cavalry officer? They don't have to do more than gallop in the right direction. And he'll bring out all of Sussex for us."

"Are we landing in Sussex?" Ned asked.

"I don't know where," Venner said. "And I don't care where, just as long as the wind changes and we can get out of port."

"A papist wind," Ned said sourly.

Every day the danger increased that King James's urgent demands to his son-in-law William of Orange would stir the Dutch authorities into arresting the rebels and impounding the three ships. Every day that they bobbed at the quayside increased their visibility.

"Surely they'll turn a blind eye to us," Venner suggested. "We've had nothing but goodwill from the people of Amsterdam. They're praying for our success in the chapels. They've fought papists for years."

Rowan appeared at his side, so soft-footed that Venner started and cursed her. She said nothing but touched Ned on the sleeve and pointed down to the twilit quay beside them. He could just make out two figures, city fathers by their rich clothes, broad beamed as barges, waddling towards them, papers in hand.

"Trouble?" she whispered.

Ned went without a word to the bridge, found the young recruit William Hewling on anchor watch, and ordered the gangplank to be drawn in and the duke and his officers informed.

"They're onshore, dining," Hewling said, looking anxiously over the side of the ship at the approaching officials. "I don't even know which inn."

Ned turned to Rowan. "Go and find the duke," he whispered. "Make sure you're not seen. Tell him not to come back to the ship until we know who these men are. Tell him he might have to get away." He caught her hand as she turned for the gangplank. "Not that way, they'll see you. Can you get down the mooring rope?"

She nodded and disappeared before his eyes. It was as if she had melted into air. One moment he held her warm hand and saw her confident smile under the shadow of her hat, and the next there were just shadows, not even the outline of her shadow, not even the whisper of her cape. He looked aft where the rocking ship was pulling the line taut and saw her for just a moment, silhouetted against the gray horizon as she slung a leg over the rail, then she was gone. The men holloing from the quayside had their backs to her as she wormed down the rope, going hand over hand with her legs wrapped around it, and jumped soundlessly onto the shore. She dropped into a low crouch and froze as Ned leaned over the side doffing his hat. "Good evening, *Mijn Heren,*" he bellowed.

On the bridge behind him he heard the quiet click of Venner arming a musket. William Hewling behind him was white as a sail.

One of the men looked up. "Are you captain of this vessel?" he demanded.

"The captain is off watch, sir," Ned replied. "May I serve you?"

"What's its name and where is it bound?"

Out of the corner of his eye Ned saw a shadow — nothing more than the torchlight flickering — and knew that Rowan was on her way.

"It is the *Helderenberg,* bound for Bilbao."

"We have information that this ship has been commissioned by the Duke of Monmouth for an invasion of England."

Ned shook his head, the image of doltishness. "Nay, I don't know anything about that," he said slowly. "We're laden with *baccalà* — salted codfish — and sailing for Spain as soon as the wind drops."

"Where is the duke?"

"What duke?"

"Monmouth! Where is Monmouth?"

"Near Wales, I believe," Ned said earnestly.

Hewling, caught off guard, snorted with laughter.

"We can do nothing without the facts!"

"No, sir. No more can I. What facts?"

The men spoke among themselves. Ned could not understand their language, but he could see the worldwide unwillingness of small-town officials to exert themselves in uncertain times.

"I cannot admit you on board unless you have papers," Ned said apologetically. "Do you have papers?"

From the exclamation of irritation from one of the gentlemen, Ned guessed that the necessary papers — in this most bureaucratic of countries — had not been provided.

"We will come back when we have the right papers," the senior man said. He brandished a handful of documents. "The English envoy failed to make the correct request."

"The English envoy tried to stop us selling codfish to Bilbao?" Ned asked, deeply shocked at the interference in trade.

"A mistake," one of the men said irritably. "And us looking like fools."

"Not at all! Not at all! Come back when you are fully certified. If you would be so gracious as to let us know when, I can make sure the captain is here to receive you."

The Amsterdam official consulted his timepiece, a handsome large silver watch chained over his broad belly. "When the envoy makes the correct application, we will return," he said. "And you are?"

"Let me give you a note of my name," Ned

said. He found a piece of paper and dipped a pen in the ink-standish. "Sir James Avery, Northside Manor, Northallerton," Ned wrote with mischievous joy, scattered it with sand to dry, tied it in the plumb line, and tossed it down to the officials.

The Amsterdammer untied the note and read the aristocratic scrawl. "Sir James?"

"At your service, sir," Ned said, reeling the line in. "Sir James Avery. Trader in codfish."

Rowan led Ned at a loping run to the quay-side inn where the duke was dining.

"I told him," she said shortly.

Ned patted her shoulder. "You did well," he said. "You went down that rope as quick as a rat." He left her at the door of the private parlor, knocked, and put his head inside the room. The duke was dining with his senior officers, Lord Grey at one end of the table, Colonel Foulness, Lieutenant Tallier, and Captain Kidd between them.

"Your pardon, sire, reporting from the ship," Ned said.

"Come in," Monmouth said. "We've been waiting. You did well to send your lad to warn us. What's happened?"

"Amsterdam officials, inquiring about our business," Ned said. "I told them we were bound for Bilbao with freight, but they've been set on us by the English envoy and they'll be back. They have to get a proper

warrant before they can impound the ship —
I couldn't understand it all, sire, they spoke
in their own language among themselves. But
I did get — loud and clear — that they'll be
back. My advice is that we sail, whatever the
weather."

"You've done me a service," Monmouth
nodded. "Ned Ferryman, isn't it?"

"We could go on the ebbing tide, at night,"
one of the men said.

"The wind's still against us," someone else
answered. "We'll struggle to get out of port."

Monmouth shook his head. "We can't wait
a moment longer." He glanced at one of the
men. "Hire barges, extra barges, to tow us
out. Once we're out the harbor we can run
before the wind wherever it takes us. But we
leave in the first lull." He rose, and everyone
leapt to their feet, calling for the reckoning
and going to their rooms for their belong-
ings. Ned, an old campaigner, quietly pocketed two bread rolls from the table and
turned to the door.

Reekie Wharf, London, Spring 1685
Matthew was not late on Friday, as he had
threatened to be. He came home early, oddly
subdued, hung his coat on the hook in the
warehouse, and kissed his foster mother.

"I thought you were out roistering," Alys
said.

"No, I wanted to come home. Is the *Sweet*

117

Hope sailing soon?"

"Next month. Why?"

"Someone asked me."

"Is everything all right, Matthew?"

He did not look at her. He thought how the other woman had called him "Matteo," as if he were someone else. "Yes."

"You've not lost money gambling?" She went straight to her greatest fear.

"No, Ma. How often do I have to say!" He checked himself at her stricken face. "No. But I'd like to talk to you and to Mother Alinor. Is she well enough to see me?"

"She's well, she's in her room."

He led the way upstairs so that she should not hurry in front of him and warn her mother that he was in trouble. Alys followed the polished heels of his smart shoes and felt her heart sinking with dread.

Matthew tapped on Alinor's door and heard her take a breath enough to say "Come in!" and stepped inside the room. He stood before her, hands at his sides, his face as blank as the beautiful statues that he resembled. Alinor raised her silver head and took him in, from the velvet bows on his shoes to the crown of his dark curling hair, noting his grave expression and the hurt in his eyes.

"Oh, you've seen your mother," she said at once.

Alys dropped into a chair as if she had been

118

winded. "Oh," she said. "Oh! Is that it?"

Matthew nodded. "She sent for me to meet her in a coffeehouse," he said.

Alinor held out her hand. "Come, my son, sit here."

He crossed the room and sank onto a stool at the side of her sofa. He leaned back, and she stroked the dark curling locks of hair from his forehead. Suddenly, he looked very young, and Alinor was reminded of the little boy he had been, the baby who had been left in their care because his mother did not want him. She laid her hand on his forehead as if she would test the heat of his skin for fever. "Go on," she said gently. He was steadied by the coolness of her hand and the faint scent of herbs in the room.

"This is my home," he said.

"It is," Alinor confirmed quietly. "No doubt of that. You've got nothing to fear, and neither does Alys. Nothing can untie the love you two have for each other. You don't have to be born a son to a mother, to be a mother and son. You two have a bond that nothing will break."

He nodded. "It's true," he said. He looked across at Alys, who was frozen in her chair. "It's true," he repeated. "Don't look like that, Ma."

"How do I look?" she demanded.

"Like I was threatening you with a knife."

"Aye," she said bitterly. "She's a sharp

119

blade. What did she want?"

"I don't know what to tell you . . ." he began.

"Better say it all," Alinor counseled. "There's enough secrets already."

"She wants a passage on Captain Shore's next sailing. She wants two berths. I said he took passengers and that he was due to go out next month as soon as she was loaded." He turned to look up at Alinor. "Was that all right to say?"

"Aye," she said shortly. "Go on."

"She told me who the berths are for — but I don't know if I should repeat it."

"For herself," Alys said harshly. "She never does anything for anyone."

"It's for herself and for the queen," he said, his voice low. "In case Argyll and Monmouth invade."

"The king's going to surrender?" Alys demanded incredulously. "He'll go like his father? Give himself up to them?"

The youth shook his head. "I don't know. That's all she told me."

"And what did you say?" Alinor prompted gently.

"I said I would ask. I made no promise." He shifted uneasily and Alinor's hand tightened comfortingly on his shoulder. "She said some other things . . ."

"Did she?"

"She said that she would serve me, take me

120

to court, that we should help each other rise in the world."

"I daresay she will serve you," Alinor spoke before her daughter could reply. "Why shouldn't she? She's your ma by birth, she'll be ambitious for you. Of course, she'll want you to do tasks for her. She's a woman accustomed to service." She felt the rapid pulse at his collarbone. "Did you like her, Matthew?"

"She called me *caro figlio,*" he said. "It means dear son."

"She said she would never take you from us!" Alys burst out.

"She hasn't done so," Alinor said steadily. "She's given him some errands to run. She can't take him, Alys. He spent his childhood with us, he's had our love poured on him. Nobody can take that from him." She smiled at Matthew, whose color had risen. "Nobody can take him anywhere — nor can we keep him. He's old enough to choose where he wants to live and what sort of man he wants to be."

"Here?" Alys turned to the boy she had raised as her own son, her blue eyes imploring in her square face. "You'll live here, in your home? As we raised you."

He rose to his feet. "Ma — this will always be my home and you're my mother."

She waited.

"But of course I want to rise in the world!"

There was a silence in the sunlit room. Outside, the gulls cried over the flowing tide, wheeled on silver wings.

"We have risen," Alys said defensively. "You've no idea what it was like here when we first came. We've risen. Through hard work. Slow but steady. Trading, little profits, well earned. Hard earned. We never sold underweight. We never borrowed, we always paid on the nail. We never issued a note of credit without money behind it."

"You didn't send me to Lincoln's Inn to come home to be a wharfinger."

"It was her who sent you," Alys said resentfully. "To turn you into a gentleman. I always feared she would spoil you —"

"I am a gentleman!" he exclaimed. "I was born a gentleman! I am descended from the Fiori family!"

"Are you?" Alinor asked.

"Yes, of course. I am stepson to Sir James Avery!"

"Was he there?"

"No. Just her. I don't know what she wants. Only what she tells me." He looked at Alys. "What am I to tell her?" he asked.

They both turned to Alinor, as if her foresight could keep them safe.

"You can tell her that she can have passage in Captain Shore's ship, if he agrees to it," she said gently. "You'll have to ask him yourself. Make sure he knows who he'll be carrying. And you can tell her when he'll sail. I doubt he'll wait for her and you shouldn't ask it of him. If we're no use to her, she can find someone else."

He nodded. "Is that all right with you, Ma?"

Alys's face was shut and resentful. "She comes to us whenever she wants something and then she goes again. Sir James is just the same. They just turn up when they want something, and they break our hearts and go . . ."

Alinor's smile at her daughter was filled with compassion. "Yes," she said. "They have to come to us, because they have so little of their own. They have to come to us, they are so poor themselves."

"I think she's very rich . . ." Matthew said tentatively.

Alinor smiled at him. "They are poor in heart."

Texel Island, Holland, Spring 1685

Monmouth was on the bridge of his ship, checking that men and stores were aboard before the gangplank was run in and the lines cast off from the shore. Extra barges surrounded the ship, lines attached, preparing to tow the *Helderenberg* out of the harbor into an onshore wind that was wheeling at last to the east, the stocky bargees spitting into their work-worn palms and predicting that it would be a hard pull. The little ships were readying themselves to follow. The Dutch pilot was beside the steersman, pointing a route through the sandbars and mudbanks, warning of the wrecks in the shallows. Tentatively, the ship rocked and then started to glide away from the dark shore studded with flickering lights from lanterns. The waves slapped loudly against the keel as the wind blew them back onshore and the barges, with their crews straining to keep the pace, fought to tow the ship out of the harbor. Ned had a familiar feeling in the pit of his belly, a mixture of excitement and dread, and knew that he was headed into battle again, surely the last battle of his life, for the freedoms of the men and women of England.

He turned to Rowan, at his side as always. "When we land, I'll give you money and you must make your way to London, to my sister's warehouse. She'll give you a bed and your keep until this is over."

He could not see her expression, her face was hidden by her hat, but her voice was clear. "I'll stay with you."

"I'll be going into battle if the king's army comes against us," Ned said. "And if it doesn't, I'll be training men. I don't even know where we'll land, but we've got to take the capital. If we land up north, up the east coast, it could be many days' march, south to London."

"Then you'll be going to London as you

say I must," she pointed out. "I'll go with you."

"Not with an army of raw recruits!" he exclaimed.

"Don't you want me with you?"

He checked his sudden denial and measured his words, conscious of her trusting gaze on his face. "Rowan, this is my mistake. I never thought we'd sail at once. I should've left you in London."

She stepped a little closer. "But as your servant . . ."

"We both know that you're not my servant. I bought you out of slavery to set you free."

"Then as a free woman, I will stay with you until the danger is past," she said.

"There's danger now," he said, looking out into the darkness where the wind was whipping up the dark sea into rolling waves with whitecaps.

"I'm not afraid of the sea," she said — a woman of the ocean who had shot the breakers of the Atlantic shore in her own canoe since childhood.

He had to stop himself reaching out to cup her defiant face in his rough palms. He wanted to draw her closer, hold her, wrap her in his old cape, keep her safe. He wondered at himself that he should have become so fond of a stranger young enough to be his granddaughter.

"I should order you to safety."

"After we land," she bargained with him. "When we see what danger there is. Order me then." She nearly trapped him into agreement.

"And you'll obey me then?"

She laughed like the Pokanoket child he remembered. "Yes! If I think you're right!"

"Very well," he said, hiding his tenderness. "You can stay with me as we march on London, unless it looks like there's danger, and then you'll go to Alinor."

"Agreed," she said cheerfully.

St. James's Palace, London, Spring 1685

To Lady James Avery,
Madam,

I have been commanded to muster the militia and prepare for an invasion by Argyll and Monmouth. I doubt that local forces will be able to hold the rebels from marching on London.

Accordingly, I am sending my carriage with outriders today, to bring you home to safety. I order you, madam, to make your excuses to Their Majesties, and come home.

Your obdt. servant and husband,
James Avery

Livia refolded the letter and tapped it, thoughtfully, against her rouged lips. Disobeying her husband would be a great risk; he had an undeniable legal right to order her home, but if she defied him and stayed, and

127

the third civil war broke out and the royalists lost — as they had done twice before — then Livia would be on the losing side, in a royal household at the time of its fall.

Whether she should take the Avery carriage and run home to safety, or gamble everything on a royal victory, was something she could not decide, though she walked up and down the queen's gallery, tapping the letter against her lips until it looked as if it were blood-stained in her hand.

The double doors opened and the queen came in, ladies around her, courtiers behind them. Her pale face was set in a rigid smile, as if she would deny her fears. She called for the card tables to be set up, and for a glass of wine; gaily, she challenged her courtiers to a game of ombre, and the musicians started to play. Livia was not deceived; she drew the queen into a window seat.

"Your Majesty — is there bad news?"

Queen Mary held up her fan to hide her words. "Our commander Lord Dumbarton is marching to Scotland with our army."

"He's just set out north, in the hopes of finding the invasion?" Livia asked incredulously.

"What else can he do? Better to march north than do nothing."

The two women looked blankly at each other. "I know nothing about warfare," Livia said.

"And now the king tells me that there are uprisings in the south also."

"What sort of uprisings?" Livia cried. "Why are they not put down? They wouldn't allow any uprising in Venice. You're not allowed to even think against the Doge in Venice. Why does the king allow it?"

"Have you heard of a town by the name of 'Taunton'?"

Livia shook her head, her sense of the huge strangeness of England all around them.

"It's beyond Bath," the queen said, as if she were describing New England far away in the Americas, over the ocean. "Farther west even than Bath. They have called out the militia against rebels there, in Somerset."

"Is the militia loyal to us there?"

"I don't think so. They sound frightened. They write to the king that there have been births of monstrous girls, and an earthquake, and three suns in the sky. They say this foretells the fall of the throne."

"I don't believe that there were three suns in the sky. How could there be?"

"It's what they're saying!" the queen repeated unhappily.

In the room before them someone threw down their cards and laughed at their bad luck. Livia cast an irritated glance before she remembered that she was supposed to be carefree. She smiled as if the queen had said something amusing. She put her hand to her throat as if she were overwhelmed, and she laughed and laughed, flicking out her fan.

The queen caught sight of the stained letter in Livia's hand. "Oh! What have you there? Is it news of our ship?"

"Yes," Livia lied smoothly. "As I promised, I have a ship for you. We need not be afraid of suns and monsters. We will be safe, whatever happens."

"We can sail away? We can go to Rome? The ship will take me to my mama, Duchess Laura, at Rome? I can tell her I am coming home?"

"Yes," Livia said boldly. "And my carriage is coming from Yorkshire. At the first bad news we will get safely away, either by road in my carriage or by sea in my ship."

At Sea, Spring 1685

Monmouth set a watch and turned in to his cabin for the night; the senior men had bunks in shared cabins, and the rest slept in corners of the hold, curled up in spaces between the cargo, or wrapped themselves in their new jackets against the onshore wind and slept on the deck. Ned and Rowan found a corner on a folded sail and made a comfortable nest. Rowan lay on her back and looked up at the night sky, the sail sometimes billowing out to hide the stars from her, sometimes dropping back when the wind eased. Ned folded his arms behind his head and watched her profile as he fell asleep.

Suddenly there was a shout from the lookout, and the sound of a cannon firing, the whistle of a cannonball and the great splash as it landed in the sea just astern. The ship rolled as the steersmen dragged on the wheel to change direction.

Ned was on his feet in a moment, Rowan beside him. The watch clanged the bell to muster the soldiers, and the lookout on the mast pointed to a yacht that had suddenly loomed out of the darkness behind them. Ned, glancing back at the quarterdeck, saw Monmouth, bare-headed, wearing nothing but a white shirt and his breeches, dashing up the companionway. Ned jumped up and ran after him, Rowan beside him. "Get down!" he threw at her over his shoulder. "Get behind the mast!"

"Ferryman!" Monmouth yelled down from the quarterdeck. "Is that the Amsterdam magistrates?"

Ned raced up to the quarterdeck and took the telescope that Monmouth offered him. He could see the pale outline of a yacht with no lights, broadside to them, ready to fire again, grappling hooks at the ready and the crew preparing to board. He focused on the flag of the States General. "Aye. Looks like they've got their warrant. That was a warning shot. They're signaling us to hove to. They're preparing to board."

"We'll run for it," Monmouth decided. "Captain, cram on sail, get us away. Ferryman — tell them a round of cannon, to keep them back, but make sure to miss. We can't sink them!"

"Yes, sire," Ned said and jumped down to the deck and slid down the ladder to the gun deck. The crew were ready, each standing by their guns, the hatches open, the guns rolled forward, each gunner waiting the command, the gun commander halfway up the companionway, ready for his orders.

"Fire to miss," Ned told him. "Fore and aft the ship. Make sure you're wide. Don't hit it."

"Aye, aye," the man said steadily. He turned and raised his voice to his crew. "Fore and aft. Wide. Everyone wide. On my word —" He glanced down the waist of the ship to see that they were all poised and ready. "Fire at will!" he yelled.

There was a roar of explosions and a rumble as each cannon spat out flame and rolled back into the ship, each gunner leaping aside to avoid being crushed by the recoil. At once they swarmed over the guns, ramming down gunpowder, wadding, and another cannonball and readied the pan for another round. Above them on deck they heard the crackle of musket fire. Ned prayed briefly that Rowan was hidden.

"Hold your fire!" Ned yelled. He peered

out through a gun port.

"Hold fire!" the gun commander confirmed.

"They've dropped sail, they're not pursuing," Ned said. "Stand by."

He waited a moment longer, and then Rowan's head appeared, leaning down into the hatchway. "The ship's turning," she told him. She was pushed aside by a tall man who scrambled down the companionway.

"And who the hell're you?" the man demanded in a strong Scots accent.

"Well done, lads!" Ned said to the gun crew. "Stand down, stand easy."

They gave a ragged cheer, rolled back their weapons, and closed the gunports. Each man cleaned his cannon, tidied his station, and closed the store of gunpowder. Ned tipped his cap to the man, obviously a gentleman, one of Monmouth's officers. "Ned Ferryman, sir."

"An' who gave you the order to fire?"

"Monmouth."

He was thrown. Ned looked around to see that everything was safe, especially that lights were out, and moved towards the ladder.

"I am in command of the gun deck," the man insisted. "I should have given the order. I am Andrew, Lord Fletcher. Commander of the cavalry."

"I must report to the duke."

"I shall report to the duke," Andrew

133

Fletcher insisted.

Ned stood back to let him lead the way up the ladder and up the companionway to where Monmouth was waiting on the bridge.

"Cannons discharged and rolled back, sire," Andrew Fletcher said.

"Thank you," Monmouth said briefly. He turned to Ned. "Will you stay up here on the bridge now, Ferryman? Take a watch. You've been of great service to me today. I won't forget it." To the steersman he said: "Set a course. Southwest coast of England. Devon."

"Aye, aye, sir."

Monmouth went below and Andrew Fletcher followed him without another word as Rowan appeared out of the darkness.

"You go and sleep," Ned said. "I'll come and find you at dawn." Obediently, she turned to go. "Were you afraid?" he asked her curiously. "When the cannons fired?"

She gave a little shrug of indifference. "The worst has already happened to me," she said simply. "Anything now is just finishing Misery Swamp."

"When your king was killed?"

"Killed by a traitor when we were already defeated. Killed before us, and his wife and son captured, and me taken with them," she said. "We'd rather have died than lose them. But we didn't die. I saw him go down, and then they took her and his son: our boy."

He reached for her and turned up the collar of her cloak as if to keep her warm. "There will be a dawn," he told her. "You're a child of the Dawnlands. It seems like very dark night now for you, but you're young, you'll see a lot of dawns — and they'll be happier than this one, I promise you."

The Coffee House, Serle Court, London, Spring 1685

Matthew, first to arrive at the coffeehouse, chose a bench seat with a high back, tucked away in the corner. Most of the customers were seated around the large central table, newspapers of the day and pamphlets scattered before them, discussing the implications of a recent judgment, and prices for legal services, vacancies for clerks, and the delay at the courts. Serle's patrons were mostly lawyers, juniors, clerks, and students seeking work. Clerks for rival chambers were seated at one end of the table, assigning cases for their lawyers; one or two clients hovered anxiously, hoping to meet their lawyers, some with sheafs of old papers hoping for free advice.

A stunned silence fell when Livia walked in and paused, savoring the attention. She looked around her as if she might buy the place outright. Mr. Hart bustled up to her, bowed, and offered to seat her; but she caught sight of Matthew rising from his corner table, and walked past the owner without a word. Her maid followed and drew out the chair as Livia put back her veil, kissed Matthew on both cheeks, and then seated herself. Her maid stood silently behind her.

Mr. Hart placed a small cup of coffee before her with a heaped bowl of sugar. Livia nodded, took a sip, and then regarded her son.

"You have spoken to the women of the warehouse?"

"To my foster mothers, yes," he said, nettled.

She smiled at his pride. "They agree?"

"I had to speak to Captain Shore, he sails in the middle of June. He will reserve two berths for you. I had to tell him who would be aboard."

"He will be discreet?" she demanded.

"He doesn't want to be mixed up in it at all," Matthew told her bluntly. "He won't speak of it, and he hopes you will not have need of his ship."

"They are royalists now?" she asked curiously.

"They take no interest in it," Matthew said. "They are loyal and law-abiding, and they don't want trouble."

"But the brother in New England . . ." She waved a hand as if to show that she could not recall his name. "He was an old Cromwell soldier, was he not? Fled abroad after his

136

defeat? He was on the other side, the wrong side?"

"I don't know," Matthew said cautiously. "It was a long time ago."

"Long before you were born, *caro figlio*," she said, suddenly turning her attention to him. "You have done very well for me. Your mother is grateful to her clever boy. You will be rewarded. You will see the benefit of serving me. Do I have to pay before we sail?"

"You do, and if you don't sail, you lose your money," Matthew said awkwardly. "I am sorry, but those are the usual terms."

She shrugged her shoulders; her dark cape fell slightly open, and Matthew could see the gleam of jewels on her breasts in the low-cut gown. "It is of no matter," she said. She nodded to her maid, who handed a heavy purse to Matthew. "This is enough?"

He untied the string and looked inside. "It is more than enough. About half would be —"

"Take it! Take it! It may be that you have to buy some things that we need, or pay a wherryman, or who knows what? But pay Captain Shore with it, and reserve our berths."

Matthew nodded and pocketed the purse.

"And if we do not sail — if all this has been a fuss about nothing, as the English do — then I will introduce you at court," she promised him. "I shall see you are rewarded whatever happens."

"Yes! Yes! It would be to repay their kindness to me. She's been like a mother to me, she and Ma. If I could get a house for them there, and they could live in comfort, restored to their home, and if it was the big house that they speak of, Mother Alinor could have her own stillroom and an herb garden!"

"Toll-loll!" she said, smiling at him. "I can ask; if that's what you really want, and if it is good enough for us, rents and so on. But it shall be in our name, not theirs. And you shall be the lord of the manor, not them. They will have no rights there, they will be your guests."

"It would be such a wonderful thing!" He was filled with enthusiasm. "I would be so happy."

She smiled. "See? You do want a reward for service! Everyone has a price, Son. Remember it. But I hope you learn more ambition. This place sounds like a lonely muddy little strand. But I will ask: if it is your choice. If the house has an estate of a decent size, and if there is a church with the living attached, and a parliamentary seat, then I shall try for it. What's it called again?"

"Foulmire!" he exclaimed. "Foulmire, near Sealsea Island, south of Chichester."

"Dismal name!"

A bell rang the hour, and then distantly, others joined in; the clock on the wall of the coffeehouse rang a silvery note, and some of the clerks gathered their papers and went out, the black sleeves of their gowns billowing. Livia rose to her feet and stood still as her maid arranged her cloak around her shoulders. "You must come to the palace when I send for you," she told him. "Come by boat and keep it waiting at Whitehall Stairs. You won't speak of this to anyone else. And you won't fail."

"I won't!" he promised her.

Her rouged lips parted over little white teeth. "And I shall see what I can get us." She smiled. "The Picci family seat."

Reekie Wharf, London, Spring 1685

The Reekie family were going to dinner on Saturday evening. Johnnie laid a gentle hand on his grandmother Alinor's arm, and held her back to ask her: "Grandma, have you heard anything from my uncle Ned?"

"I don't expect to hear from him," she told him. "He won't write until it's over."

"Is she with him?" he asked quietly.

She looked at him with interest. "Rowan? You care for Rowan?"

Though he was a man of thirty-five, he looked bashful, like a boy. "Of course not! I hardly know her. And she is . . . perhaps . . . unknowable! But I don't like to think of her in danger."

"I expect he'll send her back here if there's danger," Alinor predicted.

"He should have left her here!"

Alinor looked at the troubled face of her handsome grandson. "I think it was her choice," she told him gently. "If you care for her, you will have to learn that she thinks that no man is her master."

"I found her a place of work," he said. "I said I would befriend her."

"Did she ask you to?"

He looked rueful. "I meant to help her."

Her smile was knowing. "Some people only want to find their own way."

"Did she tell you?"

"No; but I was once a woman who wanted to find her own way." She paused. "I expect we will see her again."

"Can't you foresee?" he asked her, trying to laugh it off. "Can you foresee her coming back here?"

"No," she said thoughtfully. "I've only dreamed of her once, just once. A strange dream of a bluer sea than I have ever seen in this world, and she was in a little boat, with a boy. In my dream, she was going home."

"She can never do that!" he told her.

"Come and sit." Alys called them to the dinner table. Alinor smiled at Johnnie and took her seat between Rob and Captain Shore, as Johnnie sat down beside his mother. Alinor gave thanks for the food and blessed those who were absent that evening — "Our daughter, Sarah, and her family in Venice, and my brother, Ned, wherever he is tonight,